A GOBLIN POSTMAN CHILLER

LYNX

LEAP

PATRICIA BOW

This book was first published in 1996 by Cora Verlag GmbH under the title *Die Rache des Schamanen*, in German translation. *Lynx Leap* is the original (but revised and expanded) English text.

Goblin Postman icon created by Patricia Bow

Cover images:

"Ghostly Woods" by Peter Stevens (http://www.flickr.com/photos/nordique/3101121647/) used by permission and in accordance with his Creative Commons license.

"Lynx" by "Dynamosquito" (http://www.flickr.com/photos/dynamosquito/4411541366/) used in accordance with his Creative Commons license.

Chapter 1

THE DOOR HAD NO BELL and no knocker. Linnet tried banging with her fist on the scarred black panels, but nobody came. The house looked deserted. No lights showed, nothing moved, no windows were open.

"Hello!"

No answer.

"Anybody here?"

Nothing.

A crow cawed and the trees all around made a big, soft ocean sound. A breeze, too damp and cool for August, blew a mop of thistledown hair into Linnet's eyes. She shoved it back. "Can't even ask the neighbours," she said to the crow, the only living thing within sight. "No neighbours."

She stood in a clearing in the woods an hour's drive from the nearest town and two miles of switchback gravel road above the nearest village. This was the jumping-off place to nowhere. And if Aunt Theo didn't show up soon, Linnet would be stuck here, all alone in the dark woods.

So this was Lynx Leap. Not what she'd been expecting. She'd never heard of houses having names, except in books, and those were always old but beautiful or welcoming and often magical. Rivendell, for example. Not like this.

She stepped back a few paces, hooked thumbs in jeans pockets and looked right and left along the facade, all big grey stones. Sunset light slanted in from the west through the crowding birches and ma-

1

ples and pines, and freckled the stones with gold, not softening their faces. What, she wondered, had the builders had in mind when they'd layered those huge rocks and shaped those narrow windows? Indian raids? Man-eating bears? Mountain trolls? And why did all the lower windows have bars?

"It looks like a dungeon, not a house," she said to the crow.

And old, depressingly old. A hundred years? Two hundred? Were there even any Europeans in northeastern Ontario that long ago?

There was no lawn, not even an attempt at one. The weedy dirt patch in front of the house was clearly meant for cars to arrive and turn and leave again, and nothing else: you could see the ruts. "Or maybe they're ox-cart ruts." Linnet had never before seen a house without some sort of lawn or front yard, no matter how scrappy or small.

Even the air smelled strange here. Earthy and wet. And that windy sound made her feel cold clear through her cotton sweater and denim jacket. Odd sound, the way it swelled and died, almost like a slow drumbeat. She rubbed her arms and wished Theo would show.

She straightened up as a pang of horror hit. This was the right day, wasn't it? Friday, the fourth. On the phone a week ago, everything had been plain and clear. "I'll meet you at the bus station on Friday afternoon," Theo had said in her firm, cheerful voice. "We'll have a great time, Linnet. I promise you won't be bored."

Linnet hadn't said she was afraid she'd be bored, but maybe something in her voice had given her away. Spending the month of August in Lynx Delving, population 1,350, was not her idea of a fun holiday. But the decision was out of her hands. Her parents had decided that four weeks in the wilderness would be more enriching than the same weeks spent lying around the house reading, meeting her friends for swimming and movies and shopping, and just hanging out.

Besides, Theo was her dad's only sister and none of them had seen her in years.

This morning they'd packed her onto the bus in Toronto and casually waved goodbye. Six hours later she'd climbed stiffly from the bus and watched it rumble away, leaving her standing beside a pile of bags and suitcases in front of a tiny brick hut that called itself a bus terminal. There was nobody in the hut. There was no Aunt Theodora, either.

Linnet sat on her suitcases for half an hour in front of the terminal, watching the sun sink and the occasional pickup truck bounce past along the dusty road. Then she marched across the street to where the lone taxi waited. The man looked sleepily out of his open window.

"I'm Linnet Fox," Linnet said. "My aunt is Theodora Fox. D'you know her?"

"Uh-huh." His eyes opened a millimetre wider.

"Then take me where she is, please."

He grunted an Okay, carried the two heaviest bags to the car, waited while Linnet packed the rest into the trunk, slammed the trunk lid, then stopped with his hand on the door handle. "You mean her house?"

"Is that where she is?"

"Well, no. Since what happened this morning." The man scratched his neck. "She'd be up near Lynx Leap, I guess."

"Lynx Leap? What's that?"

"A house."

"Okay, take me there. Right now, if you please," Linnet said in what she felt was a good imitation of Theo's no-nonsense tone. She was too tired to ask what had happened that morning, or where Lynx Leap was. Every bone in her body ached. She was even too tired—

and felt too lost, though she'd never admit it—to complain of being hungry.

The no-nonsense tone worked. The driver asked no more questions. He drove up the winding forest road and along the crooked lane that ended at Lynx Leap, and got out and piled the luggage by the front door. As soon as the fare touched his palm he was back in the car and on his way, tires spitting gravel.

"Hey!" Linnet shouted. "Wait till I see if she's here!"

Too late. Gone.

So here she was stuck in front of this deserted heap of stone in the woods, and sunset was fading towards dusk, and she was all alone. She considered walking back down the road to the village, but guessed she would make it about halfway before collapsing, and be no better off. Maybe worse. There were bears in these woods, right? Almost certainly wolves, too.

She put the cab driver out of her mind, turned and walked along the front of the house northward. If she was lucky enough to find an unlocked door and then a telephone, surely nobody would mind her going in. It wouldn't be burglary, would it? It would be a matter of survival.

As she turned right around the corner of the house, the wind/ocean sound that had puzzled her swelled to a roar. A few strides away the ground vanished. Mist rose from the gap.

So this was what made the roaring noise. The river. The same Lynx River that flowed through the village of Lynx Delving far below. Linnet had seen it from the bus window, rippling gently under a bridge, sparkling in the sunshine.

Lynx, lynx, lynx. The name kept popping up. There was even a Leaping Lynx Motel in the village: the bus had passed it on the way in. Lynx: some sort of wildcat, right? Not very large, she seemed to

4

remember. Maybe there'd been a lot of them around here, once. She wondered if there still were lynx (lynxes?) prowling in these woods. And if they came out at night. And how large they actually were.

Up here the river was no gentle sparkler, it was a dragon trapped in a cage of rock. What a crazy place for a house! Right on the edge of the gorge, in some places overhanging it. Who in their right mind would build anything here?

A railing ran along the cliff, a flimsy affair of thin steel posts and rusty wire. A few metres upstream, a frail-looking wooden footbridge reached from one bank to the other. It looked just wide enough for one person at a time to cross.

Movement caught the corner of Linnet's eye. There was someone on the bridge, someone who had been standing so still that she hadn't noticed him. Or her. But of course it had to be Theo. Who else could it be?

Even as she turned to get a better look, the figure stepped from the far end of the bridge and vanished into the trees on the other side.

"Aunt Theo!"

No answer, no sign she'd heard. But of course she wouldn't hear, not over that pounding roar. Linnet set off at a brisk walk along the narrow path, determined to catch up before they were separated again.

The treetops at her back ate up the sun as she stepped onto the bridge. The planks felt solid under her feet, but the handrail was shaky. She walked to the centre, setting each foot down with caution, and just to prove she wasn't intimidated, stopped in the middle to look down. The water boiled black and white just metres below. Her shoe knocked a clod of dried mud from the boards. It hit the water and vanished instantly. She shuddered and walked on, wasting no time, to solid ground on the other side.

5

Past a screen of trees she found the path again. Here it was not much of a path: just a thin place in the thicket. It led both ways along the edge of the gorge, a safe two metres from the edge. Linnet turned right, back towards the house, because it seemed to her the figure had turned that way after stepping off the bridge.

"Aunt Theo! Where are you?"

No answer. But again, no surprise. This close to the torrent, the uproar would stun an elephant.

Then the trees thinned out. Linnet pushed through a tangle of sumac stems and stepped out onto a wide, flat shelf of granite jutting over the river. She was looking directly across at the back wall of Lynx Leap.

There were still no lights in the windows. The house was obviously empty, no sign of life. But somebody was watching it. The sight gave Linnet a start.

He (she?) stood on the very edge of the jutting rock: a tall figure, dark against the glowing western sky. Definitely not Aunt Theo. Linnet knew that right away, but in the deepening twilight she wasn't sure of much else.

Him or her? She settled on "him." The hair was long, but looked coarse. And although the figure was wrapped tightly in some cloak-like thing from feet to chin, the shape was too straight and angular to be a woman's, too wide across the shoulders.

He stood so close to the edge that a step would have dropped him into the furious river. Linnet couldn't see his eyes, but he was so rigidly still, it was obvious where his attention was fixed. He was staring at the house.

She took a careful step back and crouched down in the sumac thicket, making herself as small as possible. She no longer wanted to attract anyone's attention.

6

The anonymous figure put anxious questions into her head. Why stand so close to the edge? Wasn't that dangerous? What was he thinking of? Why was he watching the house that way, as if he was trying to bore holes in it with his eyes? What could he see that she couldn't?

She wanted to kick herself for being such a fool. Back in the city, where she belonged and should have stayed, she would never have been so stupid as to follow a stranger anywhere, let alone into the woods. At twilight. Alone.

There was something very weird about him. She wished she could nail it down. The last of the sunset light made a halo of the thick, coarse hair. Its silvery sheen was bright against the black rampart of the house.

For a moment, the man's right hand moved away from his side. He held something in his fingers: a long leaf-shape that caught the light along its edges, then flicked back to darkness as it turned on edge.

Linnet froze like a rabbit, not even daring to wipe away the spray that trickled from wet leaves onto her face. The mineral taste of river water filled her mouth.

A knife. He had a knife.

He wouldn't stay there forever. Any minute now, he would turn and look back. He would see her.

Oh, I wish, I wish I'd never left home!

There was still a chance. He was so tightly focused on the house that she began to hope she could sneak away without him seeing or hearing. Noise wouldn't matter; the roar of the water was deafening. It throbbed in her ears like the pulse of her own blood. Should be safe enough to move.

Yet she knew she had to move like a ghost.

Holding her breath, she stood up. Then took a silent step back, deeper into the sumac thicket. Not a leaf whispered as she eased backwards.

The man on the edge of the jutting stone turned his head and looked back. He saw her, no doubt of that. Their eyes met. His eyes....

"Linnet!"

The sound of her name came from very far away. It was like being called out of a dream. She glanced back over her shoulder and then forward again.

The man on the brink was gone. Her heart flew into her mouth and she pushed out of the thicket and ran to the edge of the rock. Still trying to stay back from the wet, curved edge, she crouched down and craned her neck to look over. Though not with any hope of seeing anyone.

The river was an explosion of rock and froth. There was no way anyone could fall into that, and live. And there was no other way down from this shelf. No path, no crevice, no steps, no handy jutting rocks or trees.

As she crouched above the cataract, she suddenly knew somebody was standing right behind her. Standing just where a push could send her flying. The back of her neck went icy.

She rose to her feet and carefully began to turn around. Then her smooth leather soles skidded on the slick rock. She flung out her arms, and the world jerked wildly around her.

Chapter 2

A ROUGH HAND grabbed her arm and yanked her back. She sat down hard on the rock and closed her eyes to make the world stop spinning.

"What the hell are you doing?" a voice yelled in her ear. "Are you crazy?"

Linnet opened her eyes. The boy crouching beside her looked about her age or maybe a year older, fourteen at most. Dark brown eyes scowled at her from under a shock of straight brown hair. Spray beaded on his hair and his knotted eyebrows and his tie.

His tie? Linnet looked again. Yes, even in the fading light she could see he was wearing a dark suit with a white shirt and grey tie, the kind of clothes her father would wear to church. Formal but ordinary. If you were in church you wouldn't look at him twice. But here in the tangled woods, above the wild water, the boy looked as strange as if he'd stepped down from a UFO.

He scowled again and opened his mouth to yell something else. Linnet's nerves snapped. "I saw a man jump!" she shrieked.

"What?"

She put her mouth an inch from his ear and shouted. "I said, somebody jumped! Is there a way down from here?"

"No!" he bellowed. "It's all undercut." He made a gouging motion with one hand. "You sure you saw him?"

"Yes!" She closed her eyes and tried to recapture the scene, but it was fading like a dream.

He'd had a knife, she remembered that. And there was something about the eyes. When she tried to picture the eyes, a queasy feeling dug into her stomach. Her thoughts darted aside and the memory was gone.

"Not many people up here," the boy yelled in her ear. "Private property! And there was no car by the house. Was it a hiker?"

She recalled the cloaked silhouette. "No."

"Mist, maybe?"

"Missed? What?" She stared at him, baffled.

"Mist. Spray from the gorge. Makes shapes sometimes." The boy was being patient, playing the calm elder humouring the fluttery little girl. That stung. He wasn't much older than she was. What stung worse, though, was that she was starting to second-guess herself.

"So, all this is your property?" she demanded. "And the woods, too? And the river? And the air?" She waved an arm sarcastically. "All yours?"

"Not mine. Ours. Not the river or the air, but the woods, yes. That is, some of it belongs to my great-uncle. I mean, it did."

"Did? What happened?"

He started to speak again, then wiped drops from his chin and waved across at the house. "Come on, Linnet, let's get back!" he shouted as he got to his feet. "They're worried about you!"

"How'd you know I was here?" Linnet rose carefully and stepped away from the smooth brink. Another thought struck. "And how do you know my name? And who are you?"

He grinned brilliantly, proving he could do something besides scowl. "I saw you from the other side. And your name's on the suit-case labels. And Mark Tanner."

He headed back along the path with Linnet close at his heels, anxious not to lose him. When they reached the near end of the bridge, he stopped and pointed downward.

"See that?"

Down in the gorge the torrent raged ghost-white against the dark rocks. A fallen boulder was visible in the dusk only because of the froth that fountained over it. It lay half out of the water and a good-sized cedar lay under it, crushed.

"They had a rainy summer," Mark shouted. "All this part of the cliff is going down, chunk by chunk. And you don't know which chunk will go next. Just make sure you're not standing on it when it goes!"

"I'm not an idiot," Linnet shouted back.

"Good to know!" They crossed the bridge in silence, Mark in the lead. Out from under the trees there was enough grey light to show that he was tall for his age and gangly, with a funny, loose-kneed way of walking. Like a stork.

As they stepped off the bridge, a white light blazed out of the twilight, making Linnet shield her eyes. Rounding the corner of the house, she saw that the light shone out from above the door. Three cars were parked on the dirt patch: a brown Jeep, a black BMW, and a black-and-white police cruiser. Four people stood in the glare of light in front of the cars.

Three of the four were tall. A man in a Sunday-best dark suit and tie like Mark's; an elegantly thin woman in a black dress and black silk jacket; and a girl, gold-blond hair slicked into a shining ponytail, also elegant in formal black, her hands and eyes on her Smartphone.

The fourth was a police officer. She looked shorter and squarer than she actually was, in a bulky Ontario Provincial Police jacket with a sergeant's chevrons on the sleeve. A peaked cap covered her hair, except for the honey-brown braid coiled into a knot at the back of her head. She was writing something in a small spiral-bound note-book.

11

"Aunt Theo!" Linnet broke into a run. Theo stuffed the notebook into her jacket pocket and opened her arms.

"Good grief! How you've grown!" After a fierce hug, she held Linnet off at arm's length and looked her up and down. "How old are you now? Eleven?"

"Aunt Theo, for gosh sakes, I'm thirteen!"

"Huh! You should be bigger. Tell Holly she's not feeding you enough."

Over Theo's shoulder Linnet saw Mark grinning. She hated being small. All her life, people had been treating her as if lack of inches meant lack of brains and guts. She'd wasted a lot of time proving them wrong: demonstrating that she wouldn't be pushed around or overlooked.

"The taxi man said you'd be here." Linnet pulled free and tried to regain her dignity. "So up I came."

"I'm sorry I wasn't at the bus terminal to meet you. The truth is, I completely forgot you were coming." Theo knuckled her forehead under the visor of her cap. "It's been a crazy week."

"You've had more than enough on your plate," the man said in a deep, musical voice. Linnet took a close look at his face, then Mark's, and told herself: Uh-huh, father and son.

"And it looks like the craziness isn't over yet," Mark put in. "Linnet, tell them about the man who jumped."

"What's this?" Theo demanded.

Linnet told the story all over again. This time she was even briefer. It was getting hard to recall what the man looked like.

"He was holding something." Something that frightened her. And there was something else, only.... No, it was all gone hazy. The only thing she remembered clearly was the way she'd felt. Scared sick. And she wasn't about to spill that in front of everybody. "And then I looked again and he was gone."

"But you didn't actually see him fall?" Theo persisted.

"Well, er, no."

"So what you mean is, first he was there and then he wasn't. Apparently."

"Um, yes, that's about it." It sounded a lot less credible told that way.

Theo reached under her jacket and pulled a flashlight from her belt. "If this person fell in the Jaws, there'll be nothing to see. But I still have to check the site."

"I'll show you," Linnet began, but Theo held up a hand. "Stay here. I know the place you mean."

"I'll go with you," Mark's father said. They walked away into the darkness.

"Why's Aunt Theo here, anyway?" Linnet asked.

"Some hiker went missing up near here," Mark said. "The police are searching the woods, with some volunteers. They had to stop when it got dark, but they'll be at it again tomorrow. Now they'll have to search the gorge, too. Because of what you said you saw on the Leap."

"What I *saw*," Linnet said evenly. Then, "The Leap?"

"That rock you were on. It's called Lynx Leap. The Leap for short."

"But I thought that was the house." She waved at it, too tired to try to make sense of things.

"The house is named after the rock. Which was here first, obviously."

"And the rock is called the Leap because?"

"Because people leap from it. It's a local custom."

"But wouldn't that be dangerous?"

"No: fatal."

The blond girl, who might have been nineteen or 20, spoke without looking up from her phone. "Mark, you're such a ghoul."

Linnet was still curious. "Leap, okay, I see that. But why Lynx Leap?"

"Not the faintest notion." Mark smiled at her, hands in pockets. Then he took his hands out of his pockets and cleared his throat. "I should tell you who everybody is, right? That there is—"

The elegantly outfitted woman, who had been glancing toward the end of the house, cut him off with a chopping motion of one hand. "Where is Felix?"

"With some of his scuzzy local friends, probably," murmured the blond girl, still texting.

"He would be! That Boyd Cray, I expect. And Jacob's taking far too long on his little jaunt, helping the police. Leaving us standing out here. Typical. I'm not waiting for either of them." She plucked keys from her tiny black purse and stepped up to the scarred front door. Over her shoulder she said, "You might as well come in, Mark. You too, since you're here." She flicked a hand at Linnet to dispense with the need for a name, unlocked the door and pushed it open. The blond girl, still thumbing her phone, followed the woman in. The door slammed behind her, leaving Mark and Linnet outside.

Linnet looked at the closed door and closed her lips on a comment about courtesy, or the lack of it. She, for one, would have held the door open for a guest. She glanced at Mark. He looked away and mumbled something that sounded embarrassed.

"I'll wait out here until Aunt Theo comes back," Linnet said. "I don't think your mother wants me around."

"My mother? That wasn't my mother!" He sounded horrified.

"Oh, sorry."

14

"That was my Aunt Alicia. If she were my mother, that would make Dell my sister." He grabbed his throat and pretended to gag.

"Dell?"

He relaxed. "The one with the phone. And Felix would be my brother. Cousins is close enough!"

"Have I seen Felix?" Things were getting complicated.

"No. Count yourself lucky."

"Ah. But that man is your father, right? And where's your mother?"

"Dead." No expression on his face or in his voice.

"Oh, I...."

"Never mind. Long time ago." He added, "Aunt Alicia is divorced and lives like a queen on her investments. Sends Felix to private schools that he keeps getting kicked out of. My dad's a science teacher at North Bay Central High School. That's where I go. Does that wrap us up?"

He had to be offended, the way he talked, but he didn't look or sound it. Linnet was unaccountably cheered to find that the icily chic woman was not his mother and the golden-haired girl was not his sister. She sat down on her largest suitcase, which was big enough for a low bench, and Mark leaned against the stony face of the house near the door. Mosquitoes zinged in. They batted them away.

"I wasn't being nosy," Linnet said.

"Yes, you were, but that's okay." He flashed his sudden grin, white in the darkness. "I'm nosy too. So you're visiting? From Toronto? I only know Sergeant Fox is your aunt. Big family?"

"No, small." She decided she owed him some information in return for his. "Theo is my dad's sister, he works with the police in Toronto, he's a psychologist, and my mom's a day care manager, and I guess they decided one kid was enough."

15

"Ah. We live in North Bay, all of us. That's about an hour's drive south of here. But I know this area. I've been coming here every summer since I was eight. I'm almost a local. Anything you want to know, anything at all, just ask." He looked at her encouragingly.

"Okay. Here's one. Aunt Theo said, 'If he fell in the Jaws.' What's the Jaws?"

"Les Machoires."

"Doesn't help much."

"That's the original French name, but most people just say the Jaws. It's the stretch of the river about a hundred metres either side of this house."

"But why?"

"Because it's the roughest, fastest part of the river. You fall in there when the water's high and, well, sometimes only bits are found. Sometimes nothing. It eats you right up. Like jaws."

Linnet thought of the tall figure who'd stood on the brink of the rock. Why had he gone to that dangerous place? How had he left without her seeing? He must have jumped, that was the only possible answer.

"Why isn't it fenced off?"

"Because Uncle Lot always said you couldn't fence off the whole wilderness, and that's what you'd have to do, to save fools from themselves."

Uncle Lot again. She began to wonder. Then she looked Mark over. "I'm guessing you weren't searching for that hiker, not in those clothes."

"No." He pushed away from the wall and stood up straight. "I was at a funeral. Uncle Lot's. He died three days ago. We think. We buried him today in the graveyard by the Anglican Church, down there." He tilted his head towards the village.

16

"Oh. I, I'm sorry." Then her eyebrows went up."You *think* he died three days ago? Don't you know?"

Mark walked a few steps away, hands bunched in pockets. Linnet could tell this Uncle Lot had been somebody who mattered. Not just some old relative, never seen, who sent a cheque at Christmas.

Mark whirled around and walked back, his eyes bright and hard. "About Uncle Lot. I've been thinking it over, and—"

Flashlight beams cut the darkness and Theo tramped around the corner of the house, followed by Jacob Tanner. Mark swallowed what he'd been about to say.

"Nothing." Theo snapped off her light. "Not a sign."

Linnet jumped up. "I did see him. I really did!"

"Oh, I believe you. It means another search." Theo sounded tired. "Now, what to do about you. I promised your parents I'd look out for you."

"But won't I be staying at your place? Like we planned?"

Theo shook her head. "It's not a good time, not now. I couldn't spare you much of myself."

"I'm not a kid! I can look after myself!"

Theo smiled crookedly and mussed Linnet's fine honey-brown mop as if she was five years old. Linnet bit back a protest.

"Why not let her stay at Lynx Leap with the other young ones?" said Mark's father.

Startled, Linnet looked over her shoulder at the gloomy stone pile, now studded with the yellow rectangles of lit windows. Stay there? Did people actually live in that house?

"Dell will keep an eye on things, and you know what a cool customer she is."

"Well...." Theo rubbed her chin.

Jacob looked at Linnet. "In case you're wondering what we're all doing here, my Uncle Lot—he was my father's uncle, actually, so my great-uncle—"

"And my great-great-uncle," Mark put in. "And I do mean 'great.'"

"Right." Mark's father smiled, the same bright grin as Mark. "He was ... well, unique. He died recently, and we're dealing with the estate: this house and a few acres of forest. Dell's studying business administration at university, so she's the perfect person to inventory the contents of the house."

"Dell has a mind like a steel trap," Mark said, solemn-faced.

His father shot him a mind-your-manners look. "Felix and Mark are here to keep Dell company and help out as needed, and meanwhile my sister and I—my sister is Mrs. Alicia Stewart, and I'm Jacob Tanner, by the way—we'll stay at the Leaping Lynx Motel in the village, while we take care of the legal side of things. It should only take a week, maybe less."

Linnet liked the way he looked right at her when he spoke, and the fact that he took a couple of minutes to explain things. As if she was worth his time and attention.

He looked a question at Theo. She pursed her lips, considering, then nodded. "That's very generous of you, Jacob."

"So, how about it, Linnet?" he asked. "Willing to take your chances at Lynx Leap?"

She hesitated only a split second. "Thank you. I'd like that very much."

Chapter 3

THEY CARRIED LINNET'S BAGS and suitcases inside. The door banged shut behind them, releasing a cascade of echoes.

The entrance hall was a stone cavern, dim and drafty and empty except for a brass umbrella stand beside the door, holding a single ragged black umbrella. From the bare flagstone floor, wide stairs curved up against the opposite wall to a landing with a tall, narrow window, then on up to the right. The only light came from an ancient-looking lamp, an amber glass globe on a brass pole, that stood near the bottom of the stairs.

Linnet rubbed her arms and looked around. It was chilly in here for August. Smelled funny, too. She thought of mildewed sheets, colonies of mice in mattresses, tattered furniture exhaling the odours of damp and old age. Imagine living here in winter! She shivered.

A distant enormous rushing sound filled the air. It sounded like wind blowing through giant pipes a mile overhead. She wondered; then remembered the river. Funny how that sound kept surprising her.

Dell and Alicia stepped out of a corridor that led away from the right-hand side of the hall. Both of them arched elegant eyebrows when they learned Linnet was going to stay. Neither smiled. Theo gave Linnet a hug and told her to be a good guest, and moments later all three adults were gone. The door banged shut again.

"I suppose I'll have to find you a place to sleep," Dell said without enthusiasm. Her tilted eyes, pale green in the yellow light, moved over Linnet's face and clothes.

Linnet returned the look. She knew she was creased, sweaty,

grimy and tousled, but after six hours on a bus, who wouldn't be?

Dell turned with a flick of her ponytail and strode to the stairs, high heels ringing on the stone floor. Linnet grabbed two suitcases and followed. Mark carried the rest of the luggage.

"Dell? Where *is* Felix?" he called from two steps below.

"Not a clue. You care?"

"No, it's just that I like it better when I know where he's at."

At the top of the stairs a dim corridor led away in both directions. Dell turned to the right, northward. All the doors were closed. The walls were white-plastered, mottled tan. No pictures. In places plaster had cracked off and stone showed through. The sound of rushing water was stronger here.

In three spots, evenly spaced, darkness retreated from islands of yellow light cast by bare bulbs in brass wall brackets. The floors were wide wooden planks, varnish long since scoured away.

Dell flung open the second-last door at the end of the corridor. "Bathroom's across the hall, sheets and blankets in the closet by the north stairs." She stepped inside, snapped a switch and waved a hand around. "There you go."

"When's breakfast?" Linnet asked brightly. "I'll help."

"Everybody gets their own breakfast." Dell stepped out, pushing Mark ahead of her, and closed the door.

"And sweet dreams to you too," Linnet growled. She looked around the room, murkily lit by an amber-shaded wall lamp near the door. A wardrobe, big enough to walk into, stood open to show empty wire hangers on a wooden rod. Dust dulled the dresser top. The mattress on the high brass bed was bare, but ... she went over, poked it, sniffed it, finally sat on it ... it seemed to be clean and dry. And no mice escaping in panic.

"This could be a very nice room if they fixed it up a bit," she said aloud. The white-plastered ceiling was at twice her height, and the floor-to-nearly-ceiling window was draped with velvet like a spill of dark blue ink.

She pushed aside the curtain, sneezed away a cloud of dust, and looked out. The room light glinted on the curls of an iron railing outside. A balcony! Linnet had never been able to resist a balcony. She looked for a latch, didn't find one; grasped the two handles and pulled the window open with a screech of rusty hinges. It divided into halves, and both halves swung inward like doors. She stepped out.

The roar of water beat up at her. A moon had risen, bright enough to show the outthrust shelf of the Leap, seven or eight metres away, directly opposite her room. Where the tall man had stood. The man with the knife.

He could have been looking at this window. The thought chilled her. She forced it away. Then she made the mistake of looking down. Her hands locked onto the railing.

The balcony floor was not solid: it was an iron lattice. A few metres beneath her feet raced a fury of black and moon-silver.

What had Mark called this spot? The Jaws. Right. Looked like a meat grinder down there. And the endless spin-past of the water was dizzying. With an effort she pulled her eyes away. It was going to take even more effort to let go of the railing and step back.

It was then that she became aware of a different sound woven into the thunder of the water. A whispery sound.

Linnet ... Linnet ... Linnet....

Somebody was calling her name in the voice the river would have used, if the river could speak. Somebody who had to be calling from the gorge itself, because there was no other place they could be.

But no one could be in that gorge alive.

She unlocked her fists from the railing and stepped back. In that

21

instant a slim figure vaulted like a cat over the railing where it connected to the wall and landed beside her, crowding her against the iron fence.

"Not planning to jump, are you, Linnet?" Laughter scrunched up his face and made him look like a malicious gnome.

She took a deep breath. Easy to guess who this was. It was harder to guess why he'd lurked in some dark doorway off the entrance hall, listening, as he must have done to learn her name, instead of coming out and saying hello. Unless this was his hello.

"How did you get here?" she shouted over the river's roar.

"Flew!" His eyes and teeth gleamed in the moonlight.

She looked past him. On this side of the house a row of balconies stretched along the second storey. Between her balcony and the next, the one Felix must have come from, lay a gap more than a metre wide. To a tall, athletic boy with enough nerve it would be a short jump. Felix didn't look like an athlete, and he didn't have Mark's length, though he could have been the same age. So he must have nerve.

"You must be out of your mind!" She stabbed a finger at the thundering water below.

"Danger! Love it! Gives me a buzz!"

"That's dumb! You could've been killed!"

"Nervous? Then why'd you let Dell put you in that room?"

"What d'you mean?"

"You mean you don't know?"

For a moment she thought he was going to leave her to stew in her own curiosity. Then he moved closer, so close that she had to back up against the railing. He bent his head towards her neck and spoke distinctly into her ear.

"About a hundred years ago, a lady named Violet Tanner had that

22

room. She was related to me. Great-great-umpty-great something."

Linnet waited, giving him nothing: because he was obviously after something.

"So, one night she came out here, and stood where you're standing." His breath tickled her ear. "And she climbed over the rail—that very rail where you're standing now—and she jumped!" He pulled back to display a smirk, then moved in again. "And they said...."

Linnet could have pushed him aside then, but a thirsty curiosity (okay, nosiness) had always been her weakness. She braced hands on the railing behind her.

"They said she leaped to her death because of *something in her room*. Something that came between her and the way out. Something horrible!"

"Something like you?"

"Hey!" The yell came from the other side, from the last balcony. Mark's gangly shape showed black against a lit window. "Is that you, Fleabites? Are you bothering Linnet? Get off there!"

"I'll leave when I feel like it, Moron!"

"That does it. Stand back, I'm coming over!"

"No!" Linnet shrieked. "Stay where you are!"

She'd had enough of this macho craziness. Felix wasn't big, nowhere near Mark's size. She could handle him.

She grabbed his arm and hustled him in through the open window and across the room. Taken by surprise, he didn't pull free until they reached the door. She pulled it open and shoved him out into the corridor.

"And stay off my balcony!"

Her last view of his face, in the narrowing gap of the closing door, told him she'd made an enemy. Hadn't scared easily enough to suit him. Too bad.

She turned the big old-fashioned key in the lock, glad it was there. Then went back to the window and pushed both sides shut. The hinges screeched again. She wished there was a lock on it. Maybe when the house was built nobody had imagined somebody like Felix.

With his nasty little story tugging at her nerves, and the image of the man on the rock like a deeper shadow in the forest of her imagination, and the river pounding outside, Linnet expected to lie awake all night.

But the big brass bed was surprisingly comfortable. The sheets and pillows and quilts she found in a cupboard near the north stairs, past Mark's door, were clean, and smelled of cloves.

Muted behind closed windows, the river throbbed like a giant heartbeat. *Pum-pom, pum-pom.*

Linnet dreamed. She woke once with a gasp of fear and then, exhausted, slept again. The dream scattered and was lost by morning.

Chapter 4

LINNET WRINKLED HER NOSE as she came downstairs on Saturday. Dust on her hand from touching the worn wooden banister, dust on the uncarpeted stone steps, dust everywhere. She was glad she had changed her favourite summer sweater and good leather flats for jeans, T-shirt and old sneakers.

A shaft of sunlight shot in through the east-facing slit window on the landing and struck diamonds. An enormous bronze-and-crystal chandelier hung from the roof of the entrance hall. Last night it had been invisible in the darkness under the high ceiling. Linnet stood and gazed. Even furred with dust and threaded with cobwebs, it was stunning. But probably it was years since it had lit up, and maybe it never would again. Sad.

The hall, like the upper corridor, was silent and deserted. She turned left from the bottom of the stairs, towards the southern corridor. An odd smell came from that direction. A smell that made her think of last year's science class. Curiosity almost overcame the gnawing emptiness in her stomach.

Then the air currents brought a different and much more delectable smell from the opposite direction. She followed it and found the kitchen at the north end of the house. Mark was standing in front of an old white-enameled range, toasting bread in a narrow wire cage over a red-hot burner.

"Led here by the nose, right?" He made astonished eyes at a pendulum clock on the wall. "Look at the time, it's nearly nine! Did Felix and his stupid stories keep you awake last night?"

25

"Not for long." She couldn't take her eyes off the toast, which was mostly golden brown and only smoking a little.

Mark switched off the burner, popped open the wire cage and tipped the toast onto a plate. "Here, dig in." He poured two glasses of orange juice from a jug and handed her one. "I'm glad you're not the nervous type. You're not, are you?"

"Of course not!"

"That's good. Because you're going to hear all kinds of stories about this place. Most of them crap."

"I'll bet." Linnet lifted her glass, then set it down again. "Most? Not all?"

Mark shrugged minimally. "I keep an open mind."

She sat down at the table, a slab of dust-free varnished yellow maple, and spread butter on the toast. "Thanks for this. Dell said we'd all have to make our own breakfast. Where is she, anyway?"

"In Lot's study, making lists. Inventorying. Not much fun in Dell. Hardly a smile. I've never heard her tell a joke, ever."

Linnet took a bite of toast and looked him over approvingly as she crunched. Khaki chinos with multiple pockets and a white sweatshirt with a classic *Star Trek* graphic on it ("Beam Me Up, Scottie!") suited him much better than yesterday's dark suit and tie. He looked less like a stork and more like a tall, restless, energetic boy.

"How often does the power go out?" She pointed to a row of kerosene lanterns on the top of the refrigerator.

"As often as the generator breaks down. Once a month, maybe."

"Generator?"

"The hydro lines don't run up here. So Lot made his own electricity. There's a cranky old coal-eating contraption that lives in a shed at the other end of the house." He smiled. "Whenever Dad tried to get Lot to upgrade it, the old man would say he wasn't going to

26

waste good money on anything that might outlast him."

"Maybe he couldn't afford it?"

"Dad offered to pay. Lot just hated to see money spent."

He opened the refrigerator, a squat, round-shouldered model that looked as if it might have stood there since the Second World War. "What would you say to fried eggs and bacon?"

She grinned. "I'd say—"

His hand flew up to silence her. He stood still a moment, listening, then soundlessly closed the fridge door.

Linnet strained her ears. She heard nothing beyond the throaty voice of the river. Mark took two soft steps to a rough plank door in the corner next to the refrigerator, turned the knob silently and eased the door ajar. It opened on a stairwell. Bare wooden steps led up and down. Darkness swallowed both flights.

Now Linnet could hear it, too. She slid up out of her chair. The sounds came from below: a clink of metal on stone, and the scrape of a shoe sole on a gritty surface. Then sudden silence, with a breathless quality, as if they, whoever they were, knew someone up above was listening.

Mark reached up and back, picked a big rubber-sheathed flashlight from the top of the refrigerator, and started down the stairs on tiptoe. It was a crazy thing to do. Violent TV-inspired images flipped through Linnet's mind in the half-second before she grabbed his shoulder.

He twitched out of her grip and took another step down. From below came quick footsteps, then a wooden thud, then silence again. Mark hissed through his teeth, switched on the flashlight and thumped down the stairs. Linnet followed him down into the fractured darkness, her heart beating fast.

27

THE CELLAR WAS A LONG BOX gouged out of wet stone. It looked as if part of it might have been a natural cave before the house was built. The walls were solid rock, with tool marks showing where outcrops had been pared away. Twelve-inch-square beams held up a plank ceiling, the under layer of the flagstone floor on the ground storey. The beams were so low, Mark had to stoop as he walked.

At the bottom of the stairs he looked around with more caution than Linnet had expected. "Okay, we know you're here! Come on out!" He ran the beam of the flashlight from one end of the space to the other. It skipped over boxes and bounced off the dully gleaming side of something large and metal: the furnace, Linnet guessed. It glistened on walls striped with water tracks like tears.

Nothing happened. No faces looked out. The only sound came from water: a constant trickling, and beneath that the growl of the Lynx River in its gorge. The stone floor vibrated under Linnet's feet. She looked down uneasily. Rivulets ran from the land side across to the river side, where they flowed into a groove in the stone and gurgled out a drain covered by an iron grate.

"Stop fooling around and show us who you are!" Mark's voice rang out, calm and confident. Then he caught Linnet's eyes and flashed her a tight grin, and she knew he was just as jumpy as she was.

Cautiously, he stepped around the bulk of the furnace. Linnet picked up a chunk of brick from the base of one wall and tiptoed after him. The light sent the shadows reeling backward. In ten slow seconds they circled the furnace, ducking under pipes. Nobody there.

They gave up the cat-and-mouse game then. Within minutes they were in and out of all the dark corners. Mark pushed up the heavy lid of the coal bin and poked the light inside. Nothing bigger than a centipede crawled out.

28

"Gone." Linnet tossed her brick away with a clatter. "But where'd they get to?"

"Only one place they could've gone." Mark swung his light to the end of the cellar farthest from the stairs. A plank wall had been built across the space at that end, and in the wall was a door. Water trickled from under it. He stepped up close to the door, hovered, then snatched it open and shone the beam inside. Then leaned forward, one hand on the jamb, and swept the room beyond with light. Linnet looked in over his shoulder.

The light glittered on water half an inch deep. The surface of the water was alive with moving rings, expanding and contracting and intersecting.

Linnet pointed. "Doesn't that make you think of *Jurassic Park*?"

"Yeah. Only it's not a dinosaur causing it, it's vibrations from the river."

"I figured."

"Still, it would be very cool if it wasn't so...." Mark let the thought hang. Linnet finished it silently. *So worrisome.*

It seemed obvious that nobody was here, either. They sloshed into the room and looked around. The space was empty. Nothing was stored here. Mark's light moved over the walls and stopped short, snagged by a vertical crack in one corner.

"That could be it!" His voice cracked with excitement.

"Be what?"

"The way they got out. And in. The unofficial back door to Lynx Leap."

From here it just looked like a crooked black line. "That? No way!"

But when they crossed to the corner, she saw how the wall's unevenness and the bad lighting had hidden most of the crack.

29

A vertical ridge created a baffle, fooling the eye. Behind it was an opening just wide enough to let a person through. A kid, a girl, a smallish teen, Linnet judged. For a grown man it would be a squeeze, maybe impossible, unless he was really thin.

Mark shone his light into the crevice. Linnet pressed close to look. The light struck a twist of rock two metres inside, but you could tell the tunnel continued beyond that.

She put her head close to the black slot. It breathed cold on her cheek. There was a faint smell of ... what? Unfamiliar. She pictured mushrooms in the dark, underground rivers. Deep empty spaces where you could wander lost forever. She bent her head closer. The crevice murmured like a sea shell. There was a rhythm to the murmuring, a regular *pum-pom, pum-pom*, like a slow and distant drum beat. And a soft sound that might have been far-off singing.

The longer she listened, she surer she grew. "I've heard that somewhere before."

"Linnet?" Mark was shaking her shoulder. "What do you hear?"

"I don't know. Don't you hear it?"

He stuck his head in over top of hers and listened hard. "Just the river."

"Don't you hear that beat? That singing? Could there be somebody in there?"

"This place is playing tricks on your ears!"

"What about your burglars?"

He laughed. "They wouldn't be drumming and singing, I don't think. It's just the river."

"I guess." She felt relieved. But when he started to push through the opening, she grabbed a fistful of his sweatshirt. "You're not going in there!"

He thought about it, then made a face. "Yeah, you're right.

30

Pointless. They'll be long gone by now."

"Besides, you'd need all kinds of equipment: ropes and spikes and whatever else cavers use."

"Spelunkers. Okay, I'm not going! You can let go of me." But he kept staring at the crack. "I wish I knew where it goes. Out to the woods, I bet. The area's honeycombed with pits and caves. It's all the erosion."

"Who were these people, anyway? Kids? Or spelunkers?"

"Something more than that. Let's go, my feet are freezing."

They sloshed back across the room and out to the main cellar. When they reached the stairs, Mark ran his light up the narrow steps.

"That's where the police found Uncle Lot. Head downward."

Linnet's heart jumped in her chest. "He must have fallen."

"I don't think so. Look: we'll change our shoes, then let's walk down to the village, okay? And I'll tell you my plan."

"Plan? What plan? What are you up to?"

In the sideways glow from his flashlight, Mark looked older than fourteen. His voice was steel-hard and steel-cold.

"I'm going to catch those creeps who killed Uncle Lot."

Chapter 5

LINNET COULD TELL right away. Mark was wasting his breath.

They'd found the OPP cruiser parked on the shoulder of the road, pointed uphill, about half a mile below Lynx Leap. Theo stood beside the car, listening with a look of thinly stretched patience to a pair of hikers. As soon as she saw Mark and Linnet she gruffly excused herself, took Mark and Linnet each by an arm and walked them a few metres up the road.

"City kids," she muttered. "Too green, too much to drink, seen too many bad movies. Unbeatable recipe for panic."

Linnet looked back at them. The man and woman (or boy and girl: they could have been college students) wore identical red nylon windbreakers, khaki shorts and heavy lace-up boots. As they stood with their towering packs braced against the hood of the cruiser, they kept glancing nervously into the woods, as if they were afraid something might jump out and bite them.

Mark gripped tight the strap of his camera bag. "I've got something you need to hear. About Uncle Lot. It's important."

"It better be. I got less than four hours' sleep last night." Theo's tone was mild, but Linnet recognized the signs of temper on a short leash: tight jaw, level gaze. Quick temper ran in the family, on the Fox side. Her mother, not a Fox, was a sea of serenity by contrast to her dad.

"I know why Lot was killed. He was killed for a myth." Mark stared into Theo's eyes as if he could drill his message into her mind by sheer force of will.

"Myth?" said Linnet. "What myth?"

Theo took a breath. "Mark, there was no sign of a break-in. The house was all locked up. The lower windows are barred."

"But we found another way in," Linnet said quickly. Mark described what they'd seen and heard that morning in the cellar. Theo listened without expression.

"You see?" he demanded. "We could set a trap. We have a perfect chance to catch them, because obviously they haven't found the hoard yet!"

"Hoard?" Linnet asked.

Theo snapped, "There is no hoard!"

"Yes, but they don't believe that! That's the myth!" he whispered excitedly. The hikers, a couple of yards away, were staring. "And that means they'll come back and try again! And we can trap them!" He made a grabbing motion with both hands.

Theo took a slow breath, in and out. "Mark. I have enough to do, thank you very much, without wasting time, energy and manpower on imaginary burglars."

"But—"

"There's a man gone missing. And now those two," she jerked a thumb backward, "tell me something was stalking their camp last night and they expect me to do something about it!"

"Well, it's true. There was something stalking us," said the boy. The two hikers had quietly joined the group.

"What d'you mean? Some animal?" Linnet meant it to sound off-hand, but it came out quavery.

Theo laughed. "Don't get worried. There's black bear, moose, maybe the odd wolf or wolf-coyote hybrid around here. But nothing that wants to have you for dinner. You just need to keep a cool head in the woods." She shot a look at the hikers. "And it's not my job to

33

shoot bears for sniffing after improperly stored food."

The girl looked indignant. "We know how to store food! We hung it from a tree!"

"Good for you. My constable will have a look around your campsite, maybe today, if he finds a spare half hour. That's the best I can promise."

To Mark she said, "Remind your father about that crevice. He might consider blocking it up. No sense letting every kid in the village wander through."

"But what about my idea?"

"Grow up, Mark. Use some sense." She set them aside, gently but firmly, climbed into her cruiser and drove on up the road.

"Hick cop," the girl said.

Linnet flushed with anger. She decided Theo had been right to brush them off. Idiots!

She saw Mark staring suspiciously at the pair as they hitched up the straps of their backpacks. Then he shook his head. Face like an open book, Linnet thought. First he wondered if they could be the burglars, then decided no. Now he brightened up: he had an idea.

"Hey!" Mark hurried after the hikers as they started down the road. "What's that you were saying? Something stalking you?"

"Yeah. I still think it was human, not an animal," the boy said. "It was too tall. The eyes were at the six-foot level."

"It could've been a moose."

"Moose don't stalk you, they just barge on through. It was a man. A tall man."

The girl broke in. "No, it wasn't!" She looked at Linnet, as if for agreement. "We've been arguing about it for hours. Why would it keep circling our tent? Round and round. Only an animal would do that. A predator."

34

"Didn't you get a look at it?" Linnet asked.

"Too dark," the boy said.

The girl stopped dead, forcing the rest of them to stop in a knot on the road. "Just the eyes," she said. "That's why I'm sure it was some kind of animal. They shone."

"Shone?" Mark echoed.

"Yes, you know. Like a cat's eyes."

Ice crept up Linnet's backbone. *Eyes.* A memory slid in and out of her mind, leaving her cold.

"It was a reflection from the moon," the man said.

"Whatever. I'm not staying here another night!"

"Where was your camp?" Mark asked.

"Up there." The boy waved backwards. "Just above where we stopped that cop, for all the good that did. There's a trail blazed."

They strode off down the road, top-heavy under their packs. Mark looked back in the other direction. "I think I know the place." He was off like a race-walker, his camera bag swinging from his shoulder. Linnet scurried to catch up.

"You're actually going there? Suppose that animal is still hanging around?"

"Animal, ha! I'm betting it was our slimy burglars, looking for something to steal."

"But the eyes?"

"Theo's probably right about that," he said over his shoulder. "They watched *The Blair Witch Project* once too often."

The trail blaze was easy to find: a stroke of white paint on the bark of a big pine at the side of the road. A narrow track led past a stand of pine to a meadow of long grass sprigged with daisies and buttercups and fireweed and other flowers Linnet couldn't name. In the vertical sunshine of nearly noon the clearing was an island of bee-

35

buzzing warmth and light embedded in a sea of cool, shadowy green. Except for the bees, and a rushy whisper that Linnet recognized, after a moment, as the sound of the Lynx River gorge, the place was still.

A flattened rectangle in the grass showed where a tent had been pitched. Nearby lay a stone-circled saucer in the earth, wet and black with the dead remains of a fire. No other traces: no litter, no bits of food. Mark looked around and nodded grudging approval.

Linnet turned slowly. There were no traces of any large animal, either, at least not in the clearing. She couldn't see far into the woods. Beyond a few metres, the trunks and shrubs and grasses and thistles all fuzzed together into a green mass.

"If something really was stalking them, it probably kept under cover of the trees," Mark said. He pushed into the thicket and tried circling the clearing a metre in from the edge, shoving branches aside with his arms and scanning the ground.

Linnet stayed in the open. She felt safer there, although not by much. This sunlit meadow with its gently stirring grasses and flitting cabbage-whites seemed to nurse a secret under its serenity, like a cat that you thought was asleep until you saw the gleam in its slitted eyes.

After a few minutes Mark backed out into the clearing, flapping his arms at the cloud of mosquitoes that followed him. "Find anything?" Linnet asked.

"No. No way we'll find anything in there! But I bet it was an animal. Nothing human could survive those bugs!"

"Then let's go." She'd had enough of this place. "The constable will find your footprints. Maybe he'll think the prowler was you!"

"Kevin McKenzie? Find anything?" Mark laughed.

They started back across the clearing. Linnet walked with her head down, scanning the scrubby ground. Those shining eyes the hik-

36

ers saw must have belonged to some owl or squirrel perched in a tree, she decided.

She stopped so suddenly, Mark piled up against her and nearly knocked her off balance. "Look!" She pointed at a bare patch near the edge of the woods, a pocket of dusty earth cupped in tree roots.

"Where? What? Oh." Plain to see in the dust was a footprint. A long, thin foot with five oddly spread toes.

"What is it?" Linnet crouched beside the patch.

"I don't know. I'm no Boy Scout. I guess it must be human. It doesn't look exactly right, though. Besides, people in these parts don't go around in bare feet, not in the woods."

"Maybe it's from a bear. Don't bear prints look sort of human?" Fragmentary memories of school visits to nature interpretive centres tumbled through her mind. "I wonder what Theo will say?"

"Nothing. By the time she sees it, if ever, it'll be blown away. Or rained away."

"Take a photo!" Linnet poked his camera bag.

"Hey, right." Mark unzipped his bag. "Good thing I've got this with me." He pulled out a small digital camera.

A breeze scooped dust from the ground and tossed it in Linnet's face. She sneezed and backed away. "Better hurry!"

Mark tapped a button and the lens unfolded with a chiming sound. He aimed, moved aside to get some sun on the print, and aimed again.

Then, with a sudden roar, the trees threshed back and forth. A wave of dirt and dead leaves blew across the clearing.

When they uncovered their eyes and looked down at the patch of earth, it was swept clean.

Chapter 6

FOR NEARLY HALF AN HOUR they tramped the rutted downward-snaking road. Both were silent. Linnet was thinking about the way unsolved mysteries were piling up: oddities that might be connected, or might not. Hikers who disappeared; unidentifiable figures who jumped, or didn't, into the gorge; prowlers who might or might not be human; footprints that blew away before they could be photographed; burglars who squeezed through narrow cracks into cellars, and out again.

When the shapes of roofs and chimneys began to show through the trees below, she pulled herself back to the here and now. "Come on, Mark, open up." She tweaked his sleeve. "What was that about a hoard? Are you saying there's treasure stashed at Lynx Leap?"

He laughed: not a happy laugh. "No, but there are people who'll tell you there is. They say Lot had cash hidden all over the house. Truth is, with his books, he made just enough to get by."

"Books? He was a writer?"

"Yep. He published six books about the animals and plants and geology around here. The history, too. He knew everything about the Upper Ottawa-Mattawa region." Mark sounded proud. "I've got copies of all his books. They're good, lots of cool facts, great photos, tons of information, easy to read. But never best-sellers, I don't think."

"So, how did the hoard story get started?"

He shrugged one shoulder. "The Tanners did have money, a long time ago. They had the biggest sawmill in the county, just downstream from the house. It's a ruin now."

The road came out of the woods onto a paved two-lane highway. They stopped to let a pickup truck rumble past, then walked on down the highway, which doubled as Lynx Delving's main drag.

A cracked sidewalk appeared under their feet. They passed a log cabin with no roof and a maple tree growing inside, branches bristling out the windows. After that they passed a dump surrounded by barbed wire, a used car lot, a gas station, and a deserted "Blueberries for Sale" stand.

After another quarter-mile, a sign on a pole told them that the highway was now called Victoria Street. They passed wood-frame cottages set back under the pines, with canoes upturned in racks along the side walls. Then small stores gleaming with new paint where you could buy worms and tackle, ice cream and lottery tickets. Then, angling off to either side, streets of big old houses shaded by spreading maples and pines. Finally the busy, noisy centre of town, two blocks centred on a brand-new pink-brick and white-vinyl strip mall.

To Linnet, the village seemed to unroll like a carpet out of the woods, growing brighter and newer as it left the wilderness behind.

"Well? What happened to the Tanner millions?"

Mark sniffed. "I don't think it was ever *millions*. Whatever it was, Uncle Lot lost it all during the Dirty Thirties. You know, the Great Depression."

"The 1930s! He must've been really old!" She put a hand to her mouth. "Oops. Sorry. That sounded rude."

"No, not really. Uncle Lot was old, for sure, and proud of it. He was 98 when he died. And he would've made a hundred, I bet. He was in great shape, still went out every day to walk and check on the birds and, he said, get the good air into his lungs." His mouth tightened and he kicked savagely at a chunk of asphalt on the sidewalk, sending it skittering across the road.

"We, um, we don't need to talk about him if you don't feel like it."

"No, I want to!" He let go of the scowl and gave her a smile. "Anyway, losing that money made him go a bit strange, Dad says. He turned into a miser: he watched every penny. So, people began to figure he must have money saved up. And over the years, the story just grew."

The end unit in the new mall was a doughnut shop. Mark led the way inside. Sun flooded in through big windows and sparkled on polished plastic, glass and chrome. Linnet drew in a deep lungful of warm air. It smelled like coffee and sugar and hot fat. It smelled like heaven. Maybe Lynx Delving wasn't so bad after all.

She bought a raspberry jelly doughnut and coffee with cream. Mark ordered a chocolate glazed and a small carton of milk. They carried their orders to a corner booth by a window, looking out on the street. The shop was busy with customers coming and going, but nobody was sitting too close, and there was a high partition between their booth and its neighbour on the one side, behind Linnet's back.

"Your father," Linnet prompted, once she'd swallowed her first mouthful and brushed powdered sugar off her chin. "Couldn't he stop the stories?"

"Nope. That was Lot's fault. He kept them going. He liked to drop hints that Lynx Leap was more than it looked." Mark rolled his eyes at the ceiling. "His little joke."

"Maybe a dangerous joke."

"It was. A few years ago, some creeps from the village broke in when he wasn't there and did some damage. That's when he got new locks and put bars on the lower windows." He took a big bite of

40

doughnut and chewed furiously.

"Are you mad at Aunt Theo?"

He looked away. Then looked her in the eye. "Yes. And I'm not letting those scumbags get away with it, whoever they are. If she won't take me seriously, I'll catch them myself."

"But what can you do?"

"Identify them." He tapped the camera bag on the seat beside him. "They'll be back, you can bet on it. And soon too, because they must know we're going to get the place cleared out. And when they come, I'll be there. I'll get proof. Want to help?"

"Y-yes...."

"You don't sound too sure."

"I do want to help. But if Theo's right, you'll be wasting your time. And if she's wrong, and there really are burglars...."

An image sliced into her memory. This time it stayed instead of flickering away. A tall figure with long, coarse silvery hair haloed by sunset light. The sharp leaf-shaped flicker in his hand. The way he stared and stared at the house. The way he turned his head and saw her. Eyes that could cut stone.

With the image came a throbbing beat. A pulsing in the air, almost not a sound at all. Then the memory-image faded, but the pulsing stayed. She heard it through her skin.

"Linnet?" Something touched her wrist. She looked up into Mark's eyes, which in this bright light were the colour of mocha caramel. "Off in dreamland?"

"I was thinking." She put down her cup. "Mark, what you're planning could be incredibly dangerous. Don't do it!"

"Somebody's got to, and our wonderful cops won't. Are you with me or not?"

The drumming was rubbing her nerves raw. Yet it was so soft:

41

the stroke of a bare palm on taut-stretched leather, the pulse of blood in her ears. *What is that?*

"Linnet?"

"Oh.... Okay, yeah, I'm with you."

"Great!" He smiled at her. Then his eyes went past her and up, and the smile slid. "Oh, crap." He grabbed his head in both hands.

"I'm with you too!" Felix crowed.

Linnet twisted around and looked up to see him gloating down at her over the partition. By daylight he looked exactly like a cat. Or, more accurately, like a cat magically transformed into a boy, with his thin, bendable body and gel-spiked yellow hair and his green, slightly tilted, sparkling eyes.

"There goes all hope of keeping anything secret." Mark dropped his hands and glared.

"Not to worry! I love secrets!" Felix jumped down from the seat where he'd stood to eavesdrop and slid into the space beside Linnet.

At the same moment, a scruffy stranger dragged himself out of the next booth and squeezed in beside Mark, taking up two-thirds of the seat. Felix appealed to the stranger. "I'm good at keeping secrets, right, Boyd?"

So that was Boyd Cray. The scuzzy local friend Alicia had mentioned. Boyd said nothing. He looked like an oversized stray dog, his long mud-coloured hair shaggy and tangled, his brown leather jacket worn into shiny patches. His hands stayed under the table. Linnet guessed he was seventeen or eighteen.

That drumming sound was still in the air, soft and relentless. *Pum-pom, pum-pom.*

"Well?" Felix's eager voice rang through the coffee shop. "When do we start?" Heads turned.

"Shut up!" Mark bent forward over the table. "Forget it. There's nothing on."

"But there is, I heard you!"

"I was just mouthing off." Mark sat back, arms crossed over his chest. "Didn't mean it."

Felix opened his mouth to argue. Then he looked at Boyd, eyes narrowed. "Will you stop that!"

The drumming suddenly stopped. Linnet let her breath out.

Boyd looked startled. "Didn't know I was doing it," he said in a husky, unused-sounding voice. He brought up his hands, the left rubbing his right wrist.

"What's the matter with your pal?" Mark was cool and hostile.

"Nothing! He's just got this habit lately. He's a drummer, and a good one, right, Boyd?" Felix waggled his fingers. "Plays for this awesome group, Mister Styx. But this finger drumming all the time has been getting on my nerves."

"Mine, too," Linnet said. She caught Boyd's eyes, and for a moment he looked straight into hers, desperate and intent. He looked as if he wanted to tell her something. Then he looked away.

"Can't help it," he muttered. "Don't know where I picked it up."

"Well, stop it." Felix nudged Linnet's elbow with his own. "Hey, Linnet, I thought you had no nerves. Thought you're the girl who's not scared of anything. Hearing drumbeats in the woods now, eh?"

"Of course not. Why would I?"

"Don't waste your time on Fleabites," Mark put in.

"Drumbeats." Felix leaned close and murmured. "Deep in the woods where there's nobody."

"How can that be?" she snapped.

He smiled, cat-like. "No drummer. Only the drumming. That's how the killing always starts."

Chilled, angry, Linnet retreated into a phrase of her grandmother's. "What on God's good Earth are you nattering on about?"

"The massacres. They really happened, you know. It's history, 1892, look it up. But that wasn't the only time. It wasn't the first. And it won't be the last. It'll happen again. The drums will beat ... beat ... beat ... and the shadows will come creeping ... with knives ... out of the woods...."

A cold fist gripped her heart. Then she turned her head and caught the sparkle of laughter in Felix's green eyes.

"Thanks for telling me," she said casually. "Now you've got me interested. I'll go and find out what really happened, way back then."

"No, don't," Boyd said urgently. "Don't! Leave it alone!"

Chapter 7

"SO, THE PLAN'S OFF, is it?" Linnet asked as they stepped out of the doughnut shop.

Mark let the door swing closed. Then he headed at a brisk walk along Victoria Street. Once out of sight of the shop windows, he whirled around and laughed. "Of course not!"

"But you told Felix—"

"That was just to throw Fleabites off the scent. Not that he really believed me. He's very suspicious." He crossed the street to a block of older buildings built of age-darkened stone.

"Why do you call him Fleabites?"

"Because he's a pest and he's hard to get rid of. If I let him in on my plan, he'd turn it into a circus. Or he'd sabotage it."

"Why would he do that?"

"Well, I wouldn't put it past him to be in on the break-ins himself."

"That bad?"

"Not bad, exactly. He'd do it for the hell of it. Believe me, I know. We grew up together in North Bay. He was always a smart-ass, right from kindergarten."

"And his friend, Boyd? What's the matter with him?"

"Boyd Cray?" Mark paused to ogle a window full of second-hand cameras. After a distracted moment he said, "Nothing really wrong with him, he's just a local guy. Musician. They say he got mixed up with a bad crowd, once."

"What kind of bad?"

"Out-of-season poachers, boat thieves, cigarette smuggling. He's even been in jail. That's all over, I think. But better steer clear of him."

"Why would Felix be hanging with him?"

"Like I said, for the hell of it. And to bother Aunt Alicia, probably. She's really starched."

Linnet blew out an exasperated breath. "But why—"

Mark laughed. "You don't let go, do you? Ever think of becoming a reporter? That's what I'm going to be." He patted his camera bag. "Mark Tanner, investigative photojournalist."

"If you live that long."

He laughed again. Then his smile faded. "Sometimes I actually feel sorry for Felix. His mother's never had time for him. And before you ask why, I don't know. Maybe it's because he was always kind of runty and goofy. She's all over her darling perfect Dell, but Felix is nowhere as far as she's concerned. Maybe she's only got just so much motherly love to go around."

"That's awful!" Linnet thought of her own parents, and felt lucky. Despite their faults, nobody could say that they were short on parental love and attention. Too much, sometimes.

"Yeah, but Felix makes everybody pay. Getting himself thrown out of school, blowing off chores, staying out till all hours, getting friendly with the local low-lifes. Just to get Aunt Alicia's attention. He's a total pain in the butt! By the way, did you mean it when you said you were going to find out the truth behind those tall tales of his?"

He stopped short on the sidewalk in front of a three-storey stone building and tilted his head at it significantly. Linnet looked up at it, puzzled. Above the door was a large sign with LYNX RIVER LEADER emblazoned in gold letters on black. Underneath in smaller

46

type was printed: *Norris Urban, editor.*

"Why not? It'll give me something to do."

"Then this is the place to start." Mark pointed at the building. "The morgue."

"The morgue?" She backed away.

He grinned. "No dead bodies, just dead paper. That's the newspaper office. Didn't you know they call the old newspaper files the morgue?"

"Okay, I get it! But wouldn't the library be the best place to look?"

"Uh-uhn, the library doesn't have much. The *Leader* goes back to 1850, and they've got all the older issues on microfilm. And Mr. Urban knows me, even published a couple of my photos. Come on, I'll get you in."

Half an hour later, Linnet was sitting alone in a musty-smelling, windowless room in the basement of the newspaper building, turning the crank of a hand-operated microfilm reader.

Felix had mentioned a date. "Okay, let's find out what happened in 1892," Linnet murmured. "Ten to one it was the most boring year on record."

She and Mark had agreed to meet at the doughnut shop in two hours. He had to buy a bolt for that door in the basement. That wouldn't take two hours, so she guessed he had other errands he wasn't ready to let her in on. What exactly was he up to?

But as the reels turned and the pages slid across the glowing screen, she wasn't thinking of Mark's air of secrecy, or even of Felix's obnoxious behaviour. She was thinking of Boyd Cray.

That look in his eyes, just before he turned his head away. As if he wanted to tell her something. But there was more. He looked.... Linnet stopped with her hand on the crank. Scared stiff, that was how

47

he looked.

Why hadn't he wanted her to dig into the history behind Felix's stories? And why had he been beating out that rhythm with his fingers under the table? The same drumbeat she'd heard in the cellar. The same beat that echoed in her head even now, muddling up her thoughts. Where had Boyd heard it?

She tried to set that aside and concentrate on the words and images sliding past her eyes.

THE YEAR 1892 had not been the most boring on record. Far from it. Linnet mulled over what she'd discovered as she walked from the *Leader* office to the doughnut shop. She found Mark pacing restlessly on the sidewalk in front of the shop. He lit up when he saw her.

"Mark, you'll never guess what—"

He cut her off excitedly. "They found that hiker!"

Her heart bumped. "You mean, the man I saw on the Leap?"

"No, no, the other one. Come on!" He set off up the street at a trot. Linnet ran after him.

"Where are we going?"

"To the police station. I saw Theo drive by with a face like a thundercloud, about half an hour ago, so I went looking for news, but nobody would tell me a thing. Just that they'd found him. Maybe she'll talk to you."

The OPP detachment office was located on the ground floor of a brick building in the next block. It looked like an ordinary store front, except for the wedge-shaped logo printed on the window, with "O.P.P." sandwiched between the crown above and the Ontario crest below.

Five or six people clustered around the doorway. As Linnet and Mark ran up, Theo pushed out through the crowd and headed for her

48

cruiser, followed by her blond young constable, Kevin McKenzie.

"Will he live?" someone shouted.

Theo was expressionless. "That's for the medics to say." She caught Linnet's eye and motioned her over to the cruiser with a jerk of the head.

"Aunt Theo, what happened? Was he killed?"

"No! I'm not releasing any news yet," Theo muttered. "What are you doing with this pack of ghouls?"

"Um, I'm with Mark."

"All right, stick with him. Now, off you go, like a good girl. There's a trashy element in this town I don't want you mixing with."

The car door slammed. Linnet stepped back, fuming, as the cruiser accelerated up the road. Mark turned up at her elbow, looking pleased with himself.

"Theo treats me like a kid!" she said angrily.

"Never mind. I got some details out of Kevin, before he got in the cruiser. They found the guy in a pothole."

"A pothole?" They walked up the street westward. Puzzled, Linnet glanced down at the asphalt. "Isn't a pothole something you find in the road after a bad winter?"

"Not around here. It's a pit that's been worn in the rocks after centuries of rain. The water digs out the seams of soft limestone from the hard granite. There's lots of them near the gorge, and some of them are ten or twelve feet deep." He paused for breath.

"Sounds like you've memorized your Uncle Lot's books."

"Parts of them," Mark answered seriously. "Anyway, they found the hiker in one of those potholes, curled up like a baby and acting like he'd lost his mind. Didn't know his own name. Kept saying 'it' was following him."

"Did he fall in by accident?"

49

"Could have been accident, except for one thing."

He gripped the strap of his camera bag, bit his lip and looked solemn. Linnet suspected he knew exactly how annoying he was being.

"Well?" She poked him sharply in the ribs.

"Ow! He was missing a hand."

"A hand?"

"It could've been bitten off by a bear, Kevin said. Even a coyote." He grimaced. "Or hacked off by a knife. They can't say until the doctors've had a good look at it. But the hand wasn't anywhere around, so somebody or something took it away."

"Was it the right hand?"

He widened his eyes at her. "How'd you guess?"

Linnet didn't answer. She was too busy telling herself this had to be coincidence. A hiker who fell down a pothole in the 21st century couldn't have anything to do with the horrific events of 1892.

But telling herself so didn't keep the chill from her heart.

SUPPER WAS CANNED chicken soup, buttered toast and beans, eaten around the kitchen table. Felix didn't turn up, but Dell didn't seem worried about him. Neither was Mark.

"Felix is contrary," Mark said. "He never shows up when you want him. Then when you don't want him, he's all over you like glue."

"I keep thinking about that hiker."

"Don't worry! The guy had an accident. Just a reminder for us to be careful in the woods. Felix isn't as dumb as all that."

"But what happened to make him, I mean the hiker, make him go all squirrely?" She twirled a finger at her head.

"Probably he brought his trouble with him," Dell said, not looking up. "He was likely right on his mental edge, and getting chopped

50

up like that pushed him over." She was copying pencilled lists ("Platter, silver, 1. Forks, silver, 8. Chairs, oak, 4.") into a file on a laptop computer. From time to time she took a bite of toast or sipped from a bottle of spring water.

"I found out what happened in 1892," Linnet said in a small voice. "From those old newspapers. It was awful."

Mark put down his soup spoon and looked at her expectantly. "You mean there was actual news? Not just rumours and exaggeration?"

"There was news, all right. It started after Violet died. You know: Violet Tanner, your aunt many times removed?"

"The one who jumped from her balcony?"

Linnet nodded. "Right. From the room where I'm staying." She darted a glance at Dell, who did not look up. "Her body was found in the gorge the next day, on March 10, 1892. Couple of days after that, her brother came to Lynx Delving and got the local police to question the people at Lynx Leap. In those days the local police was just one constable. It turned out Violet had been locked up in her room the last three weeks of her life. Andrew told the constable she was unhinged, that was his word, and had to be locked away for her own good. The brother said he was lying."

Mark scooped beans and sauce onto his toast and took a bite. "What did Andrew have to say to that?" he said between chews.

"Nothing, because the next day, he was dead too." Linnet hesitated. She knew the next item would sound invented. "He was lying in the woods near the gorge, and he was missing his right hand."

Dell stopped typing to raise eyebrows. Mark stopped chewing.

"Yeah. And then there were other deaths. Fishermen, hunters. But mostly people from the village."

Mark set down his toast. "What d'you mean, other deaths? Mur-

51

ders?"

Linnet put her hands in her lap. She wasn't hungry anymore. "That was never obvious. People were found in the gorge, all battered up, like they'd fallen in and got bounced around on the rocks. Or drowned. Some were found in the woods. One man looked like he'd just had a heart attack on the road. None of them were killed by bullets or knives. They were just dead."

"Maybe it was some kind of virus."

"Well, if it was, it was the worst epidemic they ever had around here. And what kind of virus chops people's hands off?"

"You mean, Andrew wasn't the only one?"

"Every single one," Linnet said slowly, "was missing its right hand. Even the constable who tried to investigate the deaths. They found his body here, by the way."

"Here?"

"In Lynx Leap. Up in the attic. Twelve people died like that, missing a hand, inside of three weeks. And then suddenly it just stopped." She pushed away her plate, still half full. "The only one who didn't lose a hand was Violet. She was the first. She didn't fit the pattern."

"Husband killed her, I'll bet." Dell's fingers pattered on the keys.

"A serial killer must have got the others," Mark said. "Or one killer plus copycats. Did they catch whoever it was?"

"Never. All the suspects kept turning up dead." Linnet pushed back her chair and carried her dishes to the sink.

Mark joined her at the sink and scraped food debris into the bin. "Well, you can see why people would make up ghost stories about a string of unsolved murders," he said cheerfully. "When the facts aren't explained, people's imaginations work overtime." As if the words "unsolved murders" had keyed a thought closer to home, his

52

grin died and he turned away.

Linnet felt better, though, now that she'd shared the grisly story. Maybe, if she was very lucky, she wouldn't have nightmares tonight.

All the same, she was restless. When Mark announced he was going to help Dell inventory the contents of Lot's study, Linnet jumped at the chance to get her mind off the handless corpses and onto something else. "Can I help too?"

"Yes, but remember, both of you, you take your orders from me." Dell slapped her notebook closed. "Otherwise you kids will only be in the way."

Mark snorted. "I'm no kid and I knew Lot better than you did. I know all about his work. You won't know what's important and what isn't." Before she could object, he marched out of the kitchen, along the corridor, and across the entrance hall to the other end of the house.

As Linnet stepped into the study its smell pounced: a powerful mixture of dust, paper, varnished wood, chemicals and other, more organic odours. Mark reached past her to the wall and switched on a light, and the room sprang into view. It was a big room, but so cluttered with papers, stacks of cardboard file boxes, shelves stuffed with books and jars and other objects, that it looked small. You could hardly see the walls and tables and desks underneath their burdens.

The first thing to catch Linnet's eye was a shelf filled with dead bodies.

She stopped and stared. Yes, definitely dead bodies. Mice, squirrels, bats, weasel-like things, birds with beaks open and wings half spread. Not stuffed and mounted and looking pretty, just lying there dead. A long row of them, neatly arranged in a straight line.

She poked a chickadee to make sure it was real, not wood or plastic. It was real. She backed away, wiping her hand on her jeans.

53

Mark laughed behind her. "It's okay. They're pickled."

The disassembled skeleton of a large animal, perhaps a bear, was set out on a table. Nearby stood a glass-fronted cabinet displaying stone arrowheads, birds' eggs of various sizes and colours, and chunks of rock. Dell was already jotting things down on paper.

"Some of this stuff is really rare." Mark opened the cabinet and took out a slim shard of black stone, twice the length of his hand.

At first Linnet thought it was just an oddly shaped rock. Then she saw it had been worked to resemble a long leaf. As Mark tilted it back and forth, the scalloped edges glistened like glass. "It's obsidian. Lot said it might have been a ceremonial knife, belonging to the Indians who used to live on this land."

"If it belongs to them, shouldn't it go back to them?"

"Maybe, but they're all gone, cleared out years ago. Here, take it."

Linnet held out her hand and was astonished at the weight of the knife, the dense chill of it in her fingers.

Then she drew in a sharp breath, opened her fingers and let it drop. It rolled over her wrist and clattered on the floor. Blood oozed from a nick at the base of her thumb.

"Watch it!" Mark took the knife and put it back in the cabinet. "It's incredibly sharp."

"I noticed." She put the side of her hand to her mouth. When Mark tried to look at the cut, she pushed him away. "It's nothing, just a scratch."

She was trying not to think of how the knife had turned in her grip, as if it could move on its own. How it had slid and nipped like something alive: like something hungry.

Chapter 8

LINNET FOUND A TISSUE in her pocket and dabbed the cut. In a moment it stopped bleeding. She decided not to touch anything else. But then spotted something in a corner, looking like a visiting alien among these wilderness odds and ends: a desktop computer on a small table with a swivel chair in front of it. Its white-plastic newness struck a note of normality that drew her across the room.

"That knife should be in a museum," Mark was saying behind her.

"Better yet, find a rich collector." Dell tapped keys on her laptop. "There, I've made a note. We might as well make some profit from this junk."

"Junk! Don't you realize what this is?" Mark spread his arms wide. "It's Lot's life work!"

"I'd call it a whole bunch of time wasted, then."

Mark turned away angrily. Linnet called him over. She had been poking into the cartons of paper files and assorted electronic parts under the computer table and found a shoebox full of CDs and thumb drives and floppy disks, all jumbled together. "Look at this!"

"His background files. For his books." Mark flicked through them, picking things up and putting them back. "Look, he saved everything! Rain and snowfall data, temperatures, sightings of different animals, bird counts year by year...."

"Mark." She held up a small chrome memory stick.

"Yeah, what?"

"Mark," she repeated, and shoved it under his nose. He pulled his head back so he could focus. His name was on the stick: *Mark* neatly printed on a white label with black marker.

He took it in his fingers and looked it over. "Why would Lot do this?"

"Only one way to find out." She sat down at the computer and switched it on. "Okay, now it wants the password."

"No prob." Mark leaned over and tapped a series of keys.

"Wait," Dell said sharply behind him. "I've been looking for that password! How come you know it?"

"He told me, last time I was here. He said I might want it."

"Well, I want it. I need to see what he has on his computer." Dell was up and standing behind them, fingers tight on the back of the swivel chair.

"Take it easy, Dell."

"Listen, Mark. I *am* in charge! I expect you to help, not get in my way!"

Linnet gazed up at her, surprised. It was the first strong emotion she'd seen in Dell, and it looked like fury. Over a password?

"Keep your shirt on," Mark said, his eyes on the screen. "I'll write it down for you later." He pushed the memory stick into a bus port and Linnet used the mouse to open a menu.

She wasn't sure what she'd expected to find. Saved emails, perhaps. Or photos. But only one file icon showed. It was labelled with Mark's name, and a date.

"Interesting," Dell said, calm and cool once again. "That's the day before he was found."

"Must've been a letter he meant to send me, and never had time," Mark said. "But why on a thumb drive all by itself?"

"Maybe to make sure you saw it and read it." Linnet got out of the chair and waved him in. He sat, then blinked at the screen for half

56

a minute with his hands on his knees. She wondered if he was feeling as strange about this as she was. A message from a dead man.

He took a breath and clicked the mouse. The file opened. "'Dear Mark,'" he read aloud. "'When you read this, It's entirely possible that I'll be dead and gone." He stopped to breathe, then went on. "'I've had a good long run, but for a while now I've had a hunch that my time is nearly up. Before that happens, there are things you should know. I say *you*, because of all my relations you are the one with the best appreciation of what matters to me.'"

He stopped again and squeezed his eyes shut. Dell clicked her tongue. "I'll read it, shall I?"

"No! 'Unlike many others, you never believed in the existence of my fabulous hoard. Better yet, you didn't care. Well, my friend, you were wrong. The hoard does exist. And if you can find it, it's yours.'"

He broke off again and sat gazing at the screen. Linnet opened and closed her mouth.

"Well," said Dell into the astonished silence. "That proves it. Lot was right off his rocker at the end."

"He was not!" Mark flared. "He liked to pull people's legs, that's all." Then he grinned. "This was his last joke, I'll bet."

"There's more." Linnet pointed at the screen.

"Okay, here goes. 'I direct your attention to the specimens. If you look below the surface of things, you may find some answers in the story of Violet Tanner and that skunk of a husband of hers. I also urge you to explore the history of the site. If possible, speak to '" He sat back. "That's all. That's where it ends."

"It isn't finished." Linnet squinted at the bright screen. "Look at that last bit, it just breaks off."

"Something must have interrupted him."

There was a stir in the room and Linnet turned to see Felix two

57

paces behind her, his eyes sparkling with interest. Boyd hulked like a bear in the doorway.

"What's that?" Felix demanded. "What did you find?"

"None of your business." Quick and deft, Mark cleared the screen, pulled out the memory stick, and switched off the machine. Dell had already gone back to her inventory.

"What's the big secret?" Felix stepped forward, barring the way, as Mark got out of the chair. Mark just gave him an enigmatic smile, slipped the stick into his pants pocket and shouldered past, heading for the door. Boyd stepped aside, out of the doorway. Mark didn't look at him in passing.

Linnet followed, feeling she'd just seen a mime performance. Nothing said, but a lot telegraphed.

As she passed Boyd, she met his eyes and again saw that slight, eager widening that meant he was on the verge of saying something. She stopped and held his eyes. "What is it?" He ducked his head and turned away, fists in pockets. She walked on.

Twilight was thickening in the cavernous front hall as they passed through on their way to the stairs. "So you still don't believe in the hoard?" Linnet asked.

"Nope."

"What was all that about, then? About Violet, and her husband, and the specimens? Which specimens? They're all over the house!"

"They sure are! He even used the kitchen cabinets to store fossils." Mark smiled in an oddly smug way. She felt there was something he wasn't sharing with her. Again.

"And what about the history of the site?" she went on, annoyed. "And speak to who? And what could any of that have to do with Lot's hoard?"

"Nothing, of course. It's all a great big leg-pull, like I said." He set a foot on the bottom step. "But it'll be interesting to find out who's a true believer."

She folded her arms, signalling patience.

"I mean, you can bet Felix is interested. And he can't keep his mouth shut for ten minutes. If he finds out something juicy, who won't he tell? Then there's Boyd." He looked thoughtful.

"Something's really bothering Boyd." She wondered, suddenly, if it was guilt. Had he done something bad, something he was aching to get off his chest? That train of thought made her think of Lot's unfinished message.

"Mark? Dell said the date on the file was the day before Lot was found. Do they know when...." How to put it?

"When he died? The police are pretty sure it was the day before he was found." Mark looked at her distantly.

"So he wrote that message to you the day he died."

"Right. He didn't finish and we know why."

A picture formed in Linnet's mind: the old white-haired man sitting in that chair in front of that computer, typing away; then a bump or a clatter in the cellar. He stops typing, listens, saves the unfinished file and drops the memory stick into the carton, meaning to polish it off later; gets up and goes to investigate. He shuts off the computer first. Or someone else does later, mopping up loose ends.

Mark started up the stairs again. Linnet called after him. "Are you going to put that new padlock on the door in the cellar, before tonight? I'll help."

"Mm. Guess I should do that, eh?" He took the stairs by twos. Shaking her off.

Linnet turned away, sore and sorry. She advised herself not to feel bad. He was hurting. Some people got like that, when they hurt: they shut other people out.

59

But she did feel bad: lonely and unwanted. To console herself, she went in search of something to read. She was knotted up inside, questions and fears and suspicions all tangled up with the dismal strangeness of this place. She wished now that she'd never said yes to Jacob's invitation. But it had been say yes, or go home. She hadn't wanted to go home. Then.

The room across the corridor from Lot's study looked like a library: a dusty, untidy one, crammed with books on shelves and tables and windowsills, and stacked in the corners. She hoped not every single book in there was about fossils and extinct animals and other dead things.

They weren't, not all of them. One whole bank of shelving seemed to be all about history. Thinking of Lot's message, she ran a finger along a shelf full of thick old books in dark bindings. *Canada Before the White Man. Beyond the River and the Bay. The Black Robes.* She took one down and leafed through it, sneezing when dust tickled her nose. She clapped it shut—more dust—and put it back.

"Fur traders and missionaries?" she wondered aloud. "How could that possibly tell us anything about Lynx Leap?"

The shelves below were stuffed promisingly with what looked like fiction. Stuck in on top, on its side, was a beaten-up hardcover copy of a book of ghost stories. By somebody named M.R. James. On the blank leaf opposite the title page Lot had written his name: Lot David Tanner.

Linnet studied the name, thinking how people's writing so often looks like them. She hadn't known Lot but this almost made her feel she had, this firm black handwriting, slanted and scrawly yet easy to read. He looked like somebody who would be interesting to talk to.

And this book had belonged to him. One of his favourites, maybe. She thumbed through the pages, then stood there reading, ab-

60

sorbed, until a pointed finger tapped her on the shoulder. She jumped and nearly dropped the book.

"What are you doing in here?" Dell demanded.

"I'm reading." Linnet tried to sound polite, like a good guest. "I need something for bedtime."

Dell held a notebook and pencil in one hand and her laptop under her arm. "I'm starting inventory in here. What've you got?" Linnet showed the title page. Dell said, "Mm. Okay. A temporary loan. I'll note it. If I don't get it back I'll come looking for it."

"I always return books!" That didn't sound very polite, so Linnet added, "Thanks."

"Right, away you go." Dell waved her off. "But after this, stay out of this room. The door will be locked. There's valuable material in here and I don't want it messed up."

Linnet bit back something angry and impolite, walked out with her chin up, watched the door swing shut and made a horrible face at it.

Chapter 9

LINNET FELT HER WAY through endless tunnels under the earth. The darkness was absolute. She was searching blindly for the way out, groping forward with hands outstretched. But her fingers kept finding only damp rock and crumbling soil. The smell of wet earth and water was all around her, clinging to her. The soft earth clotted thick on her feet and weighed them down. Every step was more laboured than the last.

The earth was like cold flesh. Horrible, dead, rotting. Yet there was a pulse in it that throbbed whenever her hands touched it and jerked away. *Pum-pom, pum-pom.*

A sense of horror grew upon her. She wasn't alone in the tunnels. Someone was near, someone who walked in her footsteps without a sound. Someone who had the advantage, because he could see in the dark like a cat. Was that his heartbeat? *Pum-pom, pum-pom.*

Then, right at her heels, came the scrape of a foot on stone. She began to run, hurling herself recklessly into the dark. Out of nowhere a bright blade appeared in the air. It slashed at her and she fell screaming.

LINNET SAT BOLT UPRIGHT in bed, clutching her right wrist. Pain shot up her arm. She thought for a moment she was still dreaming.

Then the horror faded and the pain went with it, and she fell back onto the pillows. "Well, that's what I get for reading scary books before bed."

She groaned and turned over, snuggling for a more comfortable position. Then sat up again. "Ugh!" One end of the pillow was cold and sodden. It smelled.... She sniffed. Smelled of the river. Cool air blew in her face, bringing with it the odour of wet stone and earth and leaves.

Next moment she was out of bed and across the room to the door, feeling for the light switch. Yellow light flooded the room. The two halves of the tall window stood open to the night. The floor just inside the window was puddled.

Armed with the courage of light, she went back to the bed and looked. A wet patch covered a third of the pillow. On the sheet, close to where her shoulder had been, was a hand-sized and roughly hand-shaped mark. It was greenish black, like the algae from a fish tank. The floor was wet there, too.

"But I closed the window before bed!"

She suddenly remembered Violet, who had thrown herself in terror from that balcony. Or been pushed. A picture rose in her mind. A dark shape leaning on the bed, reaching out a dripping hand.... Then anger galloped to her rescue. She laughed. "Sorry, Violet. Of course it wasn't you!"

No ghost had done this. It was somebody alive and human. Somebody who must have a very low opinion of her, if they thought she would run scared after such a stupid trick!

First checking that the door to the corridor was still locked, she crossed to the window and closed both halves. There were handles on the inside, but not the outside. Theoretically, you could only open these windows from the inside, then.

She put a hand on one door near the handle and jiggled it experimentally. The gap between the two halves widened by a quarter inch. If you stood outside and pushed, it would probably open.

Pulling the doors open again, she stepped out onto the iron platform and looked down. The river thundered and boiled a few metres below. Had somebody been crazy enough to take the balcony route again?

She looked both ways along the face of the house. There was no light in Felix's window, but that didn't prove anything. On the other side, light leaked from the gap between Mark's curtains. So he was awake. Could Mark possibly.... No. Why would he?

She went back inside, closed the window, and stood and looked at it a moment. Then went and rooted in one of her partly unpacked suitcases, found a narrow linen sash from a tunic top, and used it to bind the two handles together, wrapping them tightly around and around. She tied it off with a double knot.

Then she looked for her sneakers in the closet. They were still slightly damp from their adventure in the cellar yesterday morning. She pulled them on, layered a purple chenille bathrobe over her pale yellow pyjamas, took a flashlight from her dresser, turned off her light and stepped out into the dim hallway.

Mark's room was the next on the right. She knocked softly, waited, knocked again. No answer. She turned the knob; the door opened. She peeked in. Mark wasn't there. The glow she'd seen was cast by a portable reading lamp clamped onto the headboard of the bed. The quilt was slightly rumpled, as if someone had lain on the bed but not slept in it. A digital alarm clock on the dresser gave the time as 2:10.

She backed out, closed the door and looked down the hall to the bathroom, but no line of light showed under that door.

For a moment she stood listening. The silence of the night intensified the booming of the gorge as it resonated through the hollow spaces overhead. This wasn't like living in a house; it was more like camping in the mountain heights. Nobody around but bears and eagles and, maybe, lynxes. No, those were probably extinct. Linnet laughed at herself under her breath.

Then froze. Another sound came from above her head: a creak of timbers. Maybe the wind, causing the house to shift? Maybe the ground settling, eroding.

No. There it came again. And again. The distinct rhythm of slow, careful footsteps. Somebody was walking, no, *sneaking* around up there, on the third floor. The storey she hadn't yet seen.

She thought about it, but not for long. No way she'd go back to bed. Not yet. If she didn't find out what was going on, she'd lie awake the rest of the night, imagining horrors.

The main staircase, in the centre of the house, went no higher than the second floor. Linnet had a choice of two others: narrow stairs, one at each end of the house. The stairway at this end, closest to Mark's room, was the one that came up from the kitchen. It was like a wooden corkscrew up the corner of the house from top to bottom.

Linnet grasped the doorknob, braced herself for a shriek of rusty hinges, and pulled. There wasn't even a squeak. A whiff of machine oil explained why.

As she climbed, one careful foot above the other, the shadows jumped up ahead of her and closed in below. At the top of the stairs there was a landing and another closed door. She switched off her flashlight and stood a few minutes to let her eyes get used to the dark.

It wasn't that dark, after all. A glowing line showed on the floorboards at the base of the door. It brightened and faded, as if someone was walking around holding a light. She stood looking at it, cranking up the nerve to push the door open.

First: listen. She placed her ear gingerly against the door panels, which were splintery and rough. Faint vibrations came through, but no sound. Perhaps she leaned too heavily. With a *snick*, the door swung open. A rushing, booming sound burst over her.

She ducked inside, eased the door closed and waited for some reaction from the room beyond. Again nothing, but a strange, unpleasant odour came to her nose. It made her think of musty old fur coats.

Squared shapes and mysterious irregular ones loomed out at her from the gloom. At the far end of what she sensed was a vast, crowded room, a yellow light glowed behind a horned silhouette. But any noise from that direction was lost in the thunder of the gorge.

Bonus! Whoever they are, if I can't hear them, they can't hear me either. And they won't notice me moving at this end, if I'm careful.

She crept forward silently. She was just beginning to feel smug about her sneaking skills when she sensed she was being watched. Instantly she crouched down and held still. Too late. Eyes were gleaming at her from only a few feet away. Pale yellow, unblinking eyes that reflected what little light there was.

Now that her own eyes were used to the dark, she could see more. Eyes were everywhere. High overhead, gleaming up at her from knee level, twinkling in the farther shadows. Eyes shining out from dim, monstrous shapes. All staring at her.

None of them moved or blinked. For the space of ten thudding heartbeats, Linnet cowered against the floor. Then she took a deep breath, swung up her flashlight and switched it on.

A snarling cat face thrust at her out of the dark.

In the frozen half-second before she reacted, the image printed itself on her mind. It was terrifyingly close. So close she could see the grey-brown streaks between the tufted ears and the individual whiskers sprouting like silver wires from the broad, speckled muzzle. Black lips wrinkled back from long, glistening fangs. A wave of hot breath stung Linnet's face. From deep in the white-furred throat came a warning rumble.

Shock silenced her for the space of a heartbeat. Then she leaped backwards with a yell. The snarling mask of the lynx vanished into darkness.

Chapter 10

THINGS HAPPENED FAST after that. At the far end of the room the yellow light winked out. Feet thudded. Linnet swept her flashlight toward the noises and caught a glimpse of Mark darting past an enormous bear. The bear didn't move.

She stood staring after him. Then understanding hit. She groaned, slapped her forehead, and began picking her way to the far end of the attic. Mark was there, sitting on a stack of books, chin in hands. He straightened up and scowled when he saw her.

"So it was you! I stay up half the night, and for what?"

"All right! I messed up! I'm sorry! But honestly, how would you have reacted if you'd suddenly come face to face with a lynx in the dark?" She brushed away a cobweb that was clinging to her chin.

She didn't mention that she'd felt the lynx's hot breath, and heard its growl. She felt stupid enough without letting Mark know how she'd panicked at the sight of a stuffed animal.

"If you'd just stayed in your room, I'd've nailed them!" He lifted the camera from around his neck and stowed it in its case. "I was almost in position for a clear shot. I waited for hours to get a picture, not moving a muscle, getting all cramped, and then you have to yell your head off!"

"Well, if you'd clued me in at the start, I wouldn't've had to go blundering around in the dark, would I? I could've helped!"

"I didn't think you'd want to help. You'd have just told me how dangerous it was." He gave her a pointed look. "You might've got Dell to stop me."

"Me go sneak to Dell! That's low! I'm no snitch!"

"Sorry," he said more mildly. "I guess you're not. Anyway, I've proved we have burglars. Remember that memory stick with my name on it? Somebody stole it from my room this evening. Right from under my pillow."

In the glow of the flashlight, his face wore a look of smug satisfaction. Linnet stared, puzzled. Then she saw his meaning.

"You wanted someone to steal it, didn't you? And I'll bet you didn't put the padlock on the door in the cellar, either. You didn't want to keep them out. You were encouraging them!"

"Not encouraging. Setting bait. And they took it. Look at this!"

He got up and led the way to where a white-tailed deer (that was what the horned shape had been, Linnet realized) stood over a heap of wood shavings and tufts of cotton. A long slash had opened the deer's belly. Someone had been burrowing inside.

"Looking for a money box, I'll bet. Something large." Mark stirred the heap of stuffing with his toe.

"So that's why they picked one of the bigger animals."

"Right. The bear and moose would've been next."

"Who were they? Did you see?"

"No, but it's a good guess one of them was Boyd. He was in the study when we found the disk. Of course, I can't prove a thing till I can get a photo."

"Felix was in the study too, and he'd've had the best chance to steal anything from your room. But he may have been too busy breaking into my room to be messing around up here." She told him about her open balcony door.

"Want me to pound some manners into him?" Mark offered.

"No, thanks. I can handle Felix. But the thing is," she added guiltily, "maybe they won't be back. Now that they know you'll be waiting."

"Oh, they'll be back. They read Lot's message: they'll be sure the hoard is here."

"Well, maybe they're right. Maybe something is here."

Mark laughed. "Are you a true believer too, Linnet?"

"No. I just think Lot would have hidden *something* for you. I mean, you were his favourite, right? He wouldn't tell you something was hidden up here if it wasn't. That would be mean."

"Yeah," he said slowly. "You're right. Even if it was a joke, he'd make sure it wasn't a lame one. He'd get that punch line in."

"But where?" Linnet slowly turned around, running her flashlight beam into the dark corners, trying to spot the perfect hiding place. There were hundreds. "This place is enormous!"

"Yeah, it covers the full length and width of the house. A hoarder's paradise."

It was more than an attic. It was a mysterious otherworld, with shadows pooled in and around an unexplored wilderness of junk. And it was populated. The sweep of the light gave Linnet an unnerving view of hundreds of heads that seemed to nod and twitch their ears as their shadows moved. Bright eyes watched her mockingly.

Mark and Linnet wandered up and down long aisles of old tables and crates, which served as stands for the stuffed creatures. Each was tagged with a label bearing its English and Latin names. Wolves, coyotes, bears, raccoons, squirrels, weasels, martens, otters, musk-rats, snakes, bats. Moose, elk and deer. Birds in their hundreds.

"Did he kill them all himself?" Linnet felt queasy. Now she knew what the funky smell was. Dead animals, gutted and preserved, and stuffed and sewn up again, their real eyes replaced with glass. As soon as she had the odour identified, she felt sick.

"Lot? Kill them? No way!" Mark was indignant. "Any specimens

Lot has downstairs, he found already dead. These are all part of old Andrew's collection. You know, the guy who was supposed to have murdered his wife in 1892? This display was famous back then. People came up from Ottawa just to see it. His aim was to kill and mount a sample of every species that was native to the region. Of course, the way they look now, he didn't do that himself: a taxidermist did."

"That's disgusting! What right did he have to kill these poor animals just so he could collect them as souvenirs?"

She was looking at a small coyote, a taxidermist's triumph. She could see now that no amateur had done this. The delicate muzzle was lifted as if to sample the breeze; the yellow eyes shone alertly. You'd expect it to jump down from its crate any moment and scamper away.

Then Mark ruffled the furry shoulder with his fingertips, and a cloud of dust puffed out. The illusion of life vanished. Only for a moment, though. When he poked his nose to within inches of the slightly exposed eyeteeth, the better to examine the lining of the ears, Linnet sucked in her breath nervously.

She couldn't get rid of the notion that the coyote was only pretending to be dead. *Use your head!* scoffed her intelligence. But the part of her that still feared the dark did not want to turn her back on this animal. Or any of the others. And they were all around.

Something stirred in the darkness at the other end of the big room. A mouse, she told herself. Or a scrap of cardboard waving in a draft. Or just the old timbers settling. If only it didn't sound so much like stealthy footsteps! There were too many feet in this place, pawed and hoofed and clawed, and none of them ought to move.

There it was again! She swung her flashlight beam at the sound and caught a glimpse of something gliding between two dressers. Something that moved with a fluid, cat-like grace.

"Mark!" she hissed. "There's something in here with us!"

He straightened. "Boyd?" he whispered back.

"Not a person. Some kind of animal. I think.... " *I think it was that lynx*, she'd been about to say, before she remembered the lynx was stuffed. Like the others, it couldn't move on its own. It had to be something else. But what live animal of that size could get in here?

"Um, d'you think," she whispered, "I mean, is it possible a live lynx or cougar could be, um, nesting in here?"

Mark swallowed a laugh. "No! And they don't nest, they den."

"Well, I saw something walking around. Something big." She pointed out the spot with her flashlight. Nothing moved there now.

As they stood watching and listening, the booming of the gorge surged in to fill the silence. Now it made Linnet think of the sound she'd heard at the crevice in the cellar. The seamless river sound had broken into that pounding rhythm, unnervingly like a heartbeat. Or was it only the pulse beating in her own ears?

And there, just at the threshold of hearing, was that whispered chant. You felt that if you only listened hard and long enough, you'd make out the words.

"You're spooked." Mark's voice, calm, normal, silenced the whispers. "You're seeing things. I don't blame you one bit."

Linnet cleared her throat. "And, and hearing things. Mark, you've been here before. I guess you know all about the, um, noises, right?"

"Noises?"

"Yes. The drumbeat sounds. And the, well, it's almost like voices, at times."

Mark made an amazed face at her across the coyote's back. "You really are spooked!"

"I am not! I'm not the nervous type. Not at all." She clasped her hands tightly.

72

"Yeah, I can tell." He sat down on a stack of old newspapers and nodded at her. "If you were nervous, though, nobody would blame you. I don't know any other house where you get sound effects like this, though Lot said you find them in some big caves. And of course there's the whispering gallery in St. Paul's Cathedral in London."

"Is it all just echoes, then?"

"Resonance, that's what Lot called it. Echoes, sympathetic vibrations, a whole slew of things. Think of a violin." His flashlight beam swirled, described the shape. "With us, the house is the sound box."

"And the river going by outside is like somebody playing the strings!" It made sense.

"Right. And probably there are hollow spaces in the cliff below us, and that would add to the resonance. And as if that wasn't enough, you get wind blowing through the leaky windows, making whistling sounds. It's not just a violin, it's an orchestra!"

Linnet wasn't sure she believed him. Whenever they stopped talking, the rhythmic sounds surged back again. But Mark's matter-of-fact manner and confident voice were the best thing for her, soothing ointment on her raw nerves.

"Okay now?" He got up and stretched hugely, waving his flashlight beam from end to end of the attic. The moving light sent shadows leaping. "Am I bushed! I'm going to sleep till noon tomorrow."

Linnet started towards the stairs. Then stopped. Mark bumped into her. "I can't shake this feeling that we're missing something," she said. "Like there really is something here."

"Maybe there is. Lot was interrupted, remember? Maybe he never got to write the punch line to his joke." His mouth tightened. "We're not done here. I'm going to help Lot write that punch line. And then we'll see who laughs."

73

Chapter 11

"SLEEP WELL?"

Linnet looked up from the kitchen range. Felix stood there smiling at her. She hadn't heard him come into the kitchen, maybe because the rain beat so loudly on the window panes. She'd been turning on the ancient burners, looking for the one that heated up red-hot, or at least hot enough to boil water for coffee. Maybe it had stopped working, like the others.

It was a dreary morning, dark and wet, but Felix looked cheerful and rested. He certainly didn't look as if he'd been creeping around the attic or vaulting from one balcony to another in the middle of the night.

"Like a log," she said. "Once I'd tied my window shut."

He made a comical face. "Now, why would you do that? Ghostly visitors? Or just bad dreams?"

"Why don't you tell me?"

"Huh?" He looked convincingly blank.

"Oh, and I had to change my sheets and pillowcase in the night."

He widened his eyes and put hands to his mouth. "Linnet! Don't tell me you still wet the bed!"

"Forget it." It was impossible to tell what, if anything, Felix really knew.

He looked in the refrigerator, said "Phooey!" and was gone again three seconds later. Ten minutes after that, Mark slouched through the kitchen door and dropped into a chair. By then Linnet had got a burner to work and a kettle to boil, and she'd found ground coffee, filters, cone, and carafe.

"Coffee? You look like you could use it."

He gave her a grateful look as she set a steaming cup on the table in front of him and a jug of milk beside that. He mixed, took a gulp, set the cup down and gasped. "What did you use for coffee beans? Burnt rubber?"

"Put more milk and sugar in," she suggested coolly.

"Where is everyone?"

"Felix is gone. To the village, I guess, for breakfast. Dell has been up and working for two hours. She's in the library with the door locked."

"Good, that means we've got freedom of movement."

"You got plans?"

He gave her a warning look, got up, went to the door and looked into the corridor. On his way back he grabbed an apple from a bowl and started munching.

Linnet poured herself a cup of coffee, put enough milk in to turn it beige, drank, and made a face which she hoped Mark hadn't seen. "I thought we had the house to ourselves except for Dell."

"Unless our prowlers come back. Listen." He beckoned with his fingers and she sat down and they leaned their heads close over the table. He lowered his voice. "I've been thinking about Lot, and I'm sure Dell's wrong. He wasn't off his rocker. The old guy was totally sane."

"Just liked making mischief?"

"Only in little things. This business with the memory stick and the message?" Mark set down the apple and spoke seriously. "This is too organized. It meant something important to him."

"Well, guess what, I've been thinking about that too." She forced down another gulp of coffee.

75

"Um?" Mark started in on a bowl of corn flakes and milk that Linnet had dished out for himself.

"I didn't sleep too well after we got back downstairs. It seems to me there were clues in Lot's letter that we could've missed."

He swallowed and wiped milk off his chin. "But the disk is gone, and I didn't copy that letter. Dumb!" He clipped the side of his head with one palm.

"Well, all the same, I think we should...."

"Yeah, me too."

AT 10 O'CLOCK IN THE MORNING, it was dark as evening on the third floor of Lynx Leap. The roof rattled like a kettle drum, and the wind squealed through the cracks. The noise of the rainstorm almost drowned out the boom of the gorge.

There were windows, but they were few and small, squares of blue light in the gloom, and mostly blocked by the heaped-up mountains of what was stored here. Linnet and Mark had both brought flashlights. The yellow beams picked out a furry hide here, a torn brocade cushion there, a bundle of 30-year-old newspapers in a corner.

In this grey twilight, the place looked even dustier and more crowded than it had in the dark. "It's like Lot's study downstairs, isn't it?" Linnet said. "Only, multiplied by a hundred."

"He hated to throw anything away."

"I can see that."

Furniture stood in islands, Victorian highboys and leaded-glass dressers next to plastic lawn chairs with ripped webbing. Around them rose reefs of cardboard boxes and dunes of magazines tied with string. Some cartons held mason jars. Linnet brushed dust from one of them and read the label. "Elderberry jam, 1953. I wonder if it's still good?"

"I wouldn't risk it."

Most of the space was devoted to the specimens. Seen by this dismal light, the menagerie was just a sad collection of stiff animal figures, with no hint of life about them. Linnet couldn't imagine how she could have been so idiotic the night before, thinking a lynx was prowling around as if alive.

"Okay," Mark began, businesslike, but Linnet interrupted him. "First, there's something I need to do."

She spent 20 minutes walking up and down the rows of tables and crates that supported the animals. Mark helped by looking under dressers and into boxes, checking every cranny where a stuffed lynx might possibly have fallen, or been pushed.

"Darned if I know why this is so important to you, though."

"I just want to know if I saw what I thought I saw, or was I completely wrong."

"Aha!" He reached under a roll-top desk and dragged out a tawny shape. "Here's your beastie!" With a grunt he heaved the big cat onto the desktop, where it teetered drunkenly.

Linnet laughed. "You kidding? Even I know the difference between a lynx and a cougar! And that isn't as big what I saw last night."

"You've got it wrong way around. Lynx aren't this big. Nowhere near. You sure?"

"Totally."

She herself didn't know why it was so important to find the lynx. But it was. She wanted to look at it, ruffle its fur, tap its glass eyes, and prove that it was just as lifeless as the others. But they never found it.

Mark had brought his camera. After they stopped searching for the lynx, he searched for evidence of last night's burglars. He spent several minutes on the dusty patch of floor beside the deer. "Useless. No clear footprints. Nothing but scuffs." He took some shots anyway.

Linnet stood looking around, chewing the side of her lip. "I wish you'd made a copy of Lot's message. I keep thinking there's a hidden joke in it."

"There would be, knowing him." Mark put away his camera in its case. "Wish I could remember exactly what it said. 'Study the specimens,' that's all I can recall."

Linnet squeezed her eyes shut. "There was something about Violet, wasn't there? He said to look below the surface of things, and study the history of the place, and talk to somebody. I wish we knew who the somebody was."

"There's no history up here, unless you count the mouldy old books and newspapers." He waved his flashlight beam. "Just animals."

"That's it: he mentioned an animal!"

"Don't think so. He just mentioned Violet and her husband."

"Yes!" She grabbed his arm. "Remember? *That skunk of a husband!*"

Mark opened his eyes and mouth wide. Then closed his mouth and set off along the aisle between the tables and crates, looking from left to right. Almost at once Linnet let out an eager cry. Mark pounced.

With its distinctive markings, this specimen was easy to spot. Mark fluffed dust from its thick black-and-white striped fur. It was a big animal, half a metre long from its nose to the tip of its bushy tail. It took up most of the space on a small marble-topped table.

"The skunk!" Linnet laughed, incredulous. "He just wrote it down, plain to see! Why didn't our burglars figure it out?"

78

"I'm guessing they aren't too smart."

Linnet ran her fingers through the fur. "Can you feel anything inside?"

"No: the hide's too stiff." He dug in his pocket and brought out a Swiss Army knife. "Sorry, Andrew."

The first slash of the blade brought a shower of cotton batting and wood shavings. The second slash clinked on metal.

They looked at each other, too excited to speak. Mark dug inside the skunk and came out with a handful of stuffing and a steel box about ten inches long. Linnet focused her flashlight on it. "Not much room in there for a fabulous hoard." All the same, her heart was beating like a metronome.

Mark dropped the skunk on the floor with a thud so he could get both hands on the box. "It's probably locked." His shaking hands fumbled with the lid. "No, it opens!"

"Let me see!" Linnet crowded in with the light. She wasn't sure what she expected to see inside. Something that gleamed or sparkled, perhaps. Instead, the light showed a brown leather bag almost as big as the box.

Mark lifted it out—it didn't look heavy—and set the box down on the table. The bag was fastened with a leather drawstring, which had aged into an oak-hard tangle.

As he tugged at the knot, Linnet held her breath. It seemed to her that the booming of the river was hushed, and all around, the animals leaned closer.

Chapter 12

"THERE!" MARK WRENCHED the drawstring open, widened the neck of the bag and thrust his hand in. Then he grimaced and pulled his hand out again.

"What is it?" Linnet was ready to stamp with impatience.

"Not sure, but I don't like the feel of it." He carefully upended the bag into the open steel box. A stiff object slid out. Linnet bent over it, then stepped back.

"So this is it? The hoard? Where did he get this horrible thing?"

At first glance it looked like a skeletal hand. Then you saw the bones were covered in skin, wrinkled and thin as brown tissue paper. Sprouting from the back of the hand were long, coarse, silvery hairs that caught the light.

No flesh remained on the thing. It looked as if it had been shut away in the dark, drying and aging, for centuries.

Suddenly she saw, with a jolt, that it was not a hand at all, because each of the five digits ended in a hooked claw, heavy at the base and narrowing to a needle-like point. "It's a paw from some animal," she said in a stifled voice. She backed away another step. The thing made her want to be sick.

"It's all dried out. Like a mummy." Mark had recovered from his first feelings of disgust. To Linnet's horror, he picked it up and sniffed it.

"Ugh, how can you stand to touch it?"

"It's just leather and bone, that's all." He slid it back into the bag, then dipped into the box again. "There's a paper under here. Maybe now we'll get an explanation." He unfolded it. "Let's have some light."

Linnet shone her flashlight on the paper. It was a lined page from a notebook half-filled with Lot's firm, hasty but precise black script. Mark read aloud:

> My father, Walter Tanner, found this object in the Lynx River gorge, downriver of the house, in 1914. He displayed it as a curiosity. Since it was found in the year of my birth, I felt some ownership of the thing (let's call it the paw): I felt it had turned up specially for me. It also made me uneasy, however, and after my father's death I stored it away.
>
> Out of sight was not out of mind. I never shed a nagging sense that I ought to do something with it: but I could never understand what that might be. After carrying out some research, I began to suspect a connection between the paw and certain events that have occurred in and around Lynx Leap over the years. I know nothing for sure, however, and now I am too old to pursue the matter, even if I had the expertise.
>
> Whoever opens this box (Mark?) may consider himself on assignment. There is a mystery here that needs unravelling: a darkness that needs to have a bright light shed on it. But be careful! Where there is darkness, there can be danger. L.D.T.

Mark lowered the page. "On assignment," he murmured. "Like a reporter."

"Something interesting?" came a cool, clipped voice from behind them.

Linnet froze, then swivelled. Dell stood there gazing at them, not quite smiling, but closer to it than Linnet had yet seen. Mark fumbled

81

with the paper, still with his back turned, then dropped the bag into the box, slammed the box shut and whirled around. Linnet lined up beside him.

"Let's see it." Dell held out both palms.

"It's not Lot's fabulous hoard, if that's what you're thinking." Mark's hands tightened on the box. "It's mine."

Dell set her feet apart and crossed her arms. Even in tank top, short denim skirt and sandals she looked pristine and formal, hair pulled into a gleaming twist at the back of her head, sculpted face unblemished ivory. Her tilted green eyes were the most alive part of her, bright with intelligence and something more. That was where she kept her laughter, Linnet saw: at the back of her eyes.

The eyes were sparkling with cold amusement now. "This is how it stands," she said, adult to badly behaved children. She pointed a forefinger. "You, Mark, have been futzing around like a conspiracy nut, first with that idiocy about Lot's death and now with this ridiculous scavenger hunt. And for what?"

Mark started to speak but she talked right over him. "Instead of helping get the house ready for sale you've got in the way of the inventory, which I can tell you is a humongous job for one person. And here you've destroyed two valuable items of property, you and your little friend."

Mark glowered. "Destroyed? What?"

"The deer and the skunk."

"But the deer was—" Linnet began.

Mark elbowed her. "The deer was a mistake," he said loudly.

"And the skunk?" Dell's pale eyes held an odd gleam in the semi-dark. "You found something, didn't you?"

"I don't have to tell you anything."

"I think you do." Again, she almost smiled. "It goes like this.

82

You show me what's in that box right now, and I don't tell Mother and Uncle Jacob that you've vandalized two family heirlooms to the tune of well over two thousand dollars."

"Two thousand dollars!" The air went out of Linnet's lungs.

"The deer, especially, is a prime piece. Or would have been."

Mark studied her face, their eyes almost at a level: he was an inch taller than Dell, although he was six years younger. Dell gazed back serenely. Mark shrugged and handed over the box. Dell opened it, lifted out the bag, checked inside the box, set it down on the marble-topped table, and opened the bag. She tipped out the thing inside and turned it over with her fingernails. "What on earth?"

"Think you can price that?" Mark's voice was edged.

"It looks like something somebody patched together for a hoax. Lot could have done it, and I wouldn't put it past him." She tilted her head. "Now show me the paper you tried to hide in your pocket."

Mark looked as if he was going to refuse again, but Dell just waited, and after a moment he dug it out and handed it over. She unfolded it, read it through methodically, flipped it to see the other side, then tossed it back. "Delusional. Poor old Lot! You can hold onto that ghastly object for now, Mark, if it gives you a kick. I'd be surprised if it's marketable."

"A thousand thanks, officer. Are we free to go?"

"Save the sarcasm." She stepped away from the table, brushing dust from her skirt. "I should still tell the parents about the damage you've done."

"Hey!" Mark jerked upright. "You said—"

"But I'm feeling generous today, so I won't. Now, get that mess cleaned up." She flicked fingers at the floor. "I'll see you downstairs inside 20 minutes. You'll be helping with the inventory, starting with the kitchen. Oh, and one other thing. You'll stay out of this storage room until I'm through with it. I mean completely out." She pivoted and clipped away toward the stairs without waiting for an answer.

"So the library's off limits, and now the attic? What's next? The bathroom?" Mark slid the mummified paw and the paper back into the leather bag. "Dell has a Napoleon complex!" he shouted towards the other end of the room. The door to the stairs closed gently.

"I think we got off easy." Linnet was down on her knees, brushing up stuffing and wood shavings with her hands. "She could've taken the box. *And* told on us." Dust puffed into her face and she sneezed. "Two thousand dollars!" She sneezed again.

"I bet they can be repaired. Leave that, I'll get a broom and garbage bag and clean it up later." He shut the box. "Now, that was weird."

"I'll say. That paw—"

"No, I mean Dell. The way she acted. I know Dell, she's all about rules. Soon as she said vandalism, I thought for sure she was going to rat me out to the parents. But she didn't. Why?"

"She wanted to know what we found. Think she's after the hoard too? Suppose that was her up here, last night."

Mark mused, then shook his head. "No. She's always laughed at the idea of Lot's hoard. It's been a kind of running joke in the family for, well, forever. Whereas Felix always perked his ears up when it was mentioned."

"Felix." Linnet picked the disembowelled skunk up off the floor. "Wouldn't she suspect?"

"Sure she would. She knows Felix as well as I do. But if she has any sisterly feeling at all, I think she might, just might, protect him if he turned vandal."

"And if she did want to protect him, she couldn't turn you in, because then you'd tell what you know or suspect."

84

"That's what I'm thinking. It's the only way to explain Dell today. She's a mystery wrapped in an enigma."

"So are we done here for now?" She ran her hands over the gutted skunk, brushing dust off its fur. "Hey! Wait." The left foreleg felt odd. It was hard, not like the other, which was stiff but yielding. "I think there's something here."

Mark glanced towards the stairs and lowered his voice. "Keep it quiet!"

Linnet wasn't happy about shoving her hand inside a dead animal, but it felt no worse than burrowing in a worn-out sofa cushion. Her hand came out again holding a glass tube of a kind she'd seen in grocery stores, usually containing saffron, or vanilla bean pods. "There's something inside: a paper, rolled up."

"Stick it in the box. We're not reading it here. Officer Dell might show up again."

Chapter 13

THEY CARRIED THEIR FINDS to Linnet's room. Mark took the mummified paw and set it on the newly made bed, despite Linnet's cry of protest, and took photos of it from all angles. "Just in case," he said. "Now, I want you to hide this."

"Me? Not you?"

"Better you than me. Whoever's after the hoard thinks I know something about it, for sure. They know I was up there last night. They're likely to try and search my room."

"Lock your door."

"That works for you, eh?"

"Well, suppose they search my room?"

"Why should they? You're a newcomer. You have nothing to do with it. You never even knew Lot."

"What about Felix getting in?" She looked at the window, where rain was still pattering on the glass.

"That was just to bug you. Anyway, he won't get through that." He tipped his head at the window handles, still tightly wrapped.

"Well...."

"Just till we figure out what it means."

MARK GRUMBLED about being assigned to inventory the kitchen, which he said was the most boring room in the house. Felix had been tapped to help Dell finish listing the much more interesting contents of the study.

"I'll help," Linnet said. "That will make it go faster." She picked up one of the foolscap pads Dell had left on the maple slab table, and looked around. "This is also one of the least cluttered rooms in the house. There's not really a lot here."

"That's because Lot didn't think it was that important. He did his real living in his library and study, and in the woods. The kitchen was just for fueling up."

"Fueling up sounds good. Let's do that."

They made cheese sandwiches and ate while opening drawers and crawling into corners to explore cubbies. After half an hour Mark, standing on the counter to reach into the back of the top shelf, let out a sudden laugh. "Call Dell! I've found Lot's hoard!"

"Really?" Linnet looked up, read his expression and rolled her eyes. "Oh, really."

"Yes, true. Look!" He lifted down a quart-sized mason jar half-full of glinting coins, then two more jars the same size. He jumped down from the counter and lined the jars up in a row. "Pennies, nickels and dimes, all sorted. Lot would have rolled them up in paper when the jars were full and taken them to the bank. See, he was serious about money, in his way."

The job took them until mid-afternoon. The completed list included, besides other items, three copper-bottomed skillets, a black iron pot that Linnet couldn't lift, an old toaster with sides that flipped up and down to turn the toast, five different metal tea strainers, a fish boning knife, a cleaver that Mark cut his thumb on testing it, a balance scale with brass weights, six bent silver spoons, and a box of tissue-wrapped tiny ceramic animals saved from Red Rose Tea.

The list also included an accumulation of small odds and ends, which they agreed to dump into a category called "Nuts and Bolts": things like rubber bands, paperclips, string, corks, buttons, and actual nuts and bolts. "And empty spice bottles," Linnet said. "Oh, and this." She reached into a drawer and pulled out a clinking handful of keys strung on a short ball chain. "Is this junk?"

Mark took the bunch and tuned the keys over in his fingers: half a dozen old-fashioned brass and steel keys with thin shafts and complicated teeth. "These are Lot's keys for the house. They look like an old set: useless, maybe." He tossed them in his hand, then stuck them into his back jeans pocket.

Linnet picked up a pencil. "Where should I put them on the list?"

"Don't." He caught her questioning look and smiled wickedly. "Dell has enough keys. She doesn't need these."

Dell came in at three o'clock to check their lists and mark significant finds with asterisks. "Not a bad job."

"Damned by faint praise," Mark said. "Felix did better, did he?"

"Felix blew it off, the pig. That doesn't let you off the hook. Tomorrow you can do the laundry room, bathroom and linen closets."

THEY HADN'T FORGOTTEN about the glass tube and what it contained. It was still in a pocket of Mark's jeans, unopened. He stood in the entrance hall, listening. There was nothing to hear but the boom of the gorge and the patter of wind-blown rain on windows.

"Not here," he murmured. "Fleabites could be lurking anywhere with his ears flapping. I know a place where nobody could possibly listen in."

Reaching that place took half an hour of squelching in single file up along narrow, twisting forest paths (deer tracks, Mark said), then fifteen minutes of scrambling up a series of rocky slopes and in and out of muddy ravines; and then a short but difficult climb up a smooth whaleback of stone.

Mark had given Linnet a choice between an oversized yellow slicker with a hood, and the broken black umbrella in the stand beside

88

the front door. The slicker looked heavy, so she chose the umbrella. Discovered that it was worse than useless in the woods when open. Closed, it came in handy as a hiking stick on the rocky slopes. When they reached the stopping place Mark offered her the slicker.

"Keep it." She flicked water drops off the ends of her bangs. "I can't get any wetter."

Now she saw what he meant about a place where nobody could listen in. The whaleback was the bald crown of the height of land north of the river. From this point they could see in all directions. On a good day the view would stretch for miles to the horizon. On this day, dark green forest faded to pale grey in the drizzle after a quarter-mile. Below them, to the south, east and west, a snake of denser white twisted through the mist: the Lynx River gorge, with its dragon of white water and high-flung spray. The nearest cover was a hundred yards away, down the hill where the forest began.

Mark pulled the glass tube from a front pocket of his jeans and they sat down side-by-side on the smooth, wet granite. "Hold the umbrella over here, will you? I don't want this to get wet." He popped off the cap and slid out a roll of stiff paper three inches long. A narrower paper was wrapped around it. Mark pulled off the wrapper and flattened it.

"What is it?" Linnet was breathless, not just from the climb.

"It's from Lot. It says: 'I found this on June 3, 1937, at Lynx Leap, while putting my late father's effects in order. It was inside a book in a box of other books belonging to Violet Tanner. L.D.T.'"

"Something he kept for more than 70 years! What could it be?"

"Looks like a letter." He unrolled and then unfolded two sheets of thick creamy paper about six by eight inches and held them tilted, to catch as much of the grey light as possible. Linnet leaned in to see.

Chapter 14

THE PAGES WERE COVERED with graceful, flowing handwriting in faded brown ink. At the top was written: *Lynx Leap, 8th March 1892.*

Mark read aloud:

My dear brother: In reply to yrs. of 4th October. You have said, more than once, that my marriage to Andrew Tanner was and is a terrible mistake; and as I have always replied, I could never agree. How well I recall our arguments on the matter! How angry you were, and how I laughed at you!

Now, dear brother, you may laugh at me. You hit the target squarely. I can admit what you say about Andrew's cold heart, for he has shown nothing but coldness to me since our wedding day. Before that his ardour turned my head completely! I have since learned that it was all moonshine; he cares nothing for me as a wife.

For me, no; but the same does not apply to my inheritance! If, as you say, Andrew was a man of straitened means who resolved to marry for gain and not affection, then he has not changed. Be assured that I do not intend to allow myself or my fortune to be abused. Nor will I accept as my lot a lifetime of silent misery, unable to act or make decisions in any matter.

I mean to seek an annulment. A few weeks ago, I began making inquiries as to the best means of regaining complete control of my income, including those parts not protected by our father's will, which Andrew has already taken.

I can no longer pursue those inquiries. I am locked in my room. Andrew learned of what I was attempting; I do not know how, but I suspect my lawyer betrayed my confidence. Confined as I am, I cannot send this letter, unless I convince one of the servants to befriend me; but they are all his bought creatures. He dismissed my maid, and she was my best hope.

But I have not given up entirely! I have a little money here in secret and may use it to buy escape for this letter, if not for me. If I succeed, and this reaches you, please, dear Fred, please come at once! And do not believe anything he tells you! He has put it about that I am deranged, and shut up for my own good. You will know whether to believe that.

In desperate need, your loving sister, Violet.

When Mark finished reading there was silence, except for the soft patter of rain on the umbrella. Linnet's chest hurt. Violet Tanner had come alive for her. She saw a young woman standing on her balcony, gazing down at the roaring gorge but not thinking of death: thinking instead of the future, and freedom. Measuring her chances, considering ways and means. And then....

"March eighth," she said. "She went off her balcony on the ninth and they found her body on the tenth. Mark, she wrote that letter the day before she died! But wait, I'm confused. Lot found it in the house, right? So—"

"So it never got sent." Mark turned the second page over. Centred on the back, in the same handwriting, was written: *Deliver to Mr. Frederick Lethbridge, 17 Albert Way, Ottawa, Ontario.*

"I can just see her hiding it in a book and waiting for the right moment to bribe one of the servants, only it never happened. Her brother turned up only because she died. If she'd got that letter out two weeks earlier, she might have lived!"

"Yeah. I know." Mark folded the letter carefully, rolled it up, re-wrapped it with lot's message, slid the roll back into the tube, and capped it. He sat turning the tube over in his fingers. "But this doesn't answer any questions. It just asks more."

"Like, why did Lot keep this for so long, and why did he keep it secret?"

"It was important to him, that's obvious. I guess it does make it seem more likely that Andrew murdered Violet. That makes it a re-ally nasty bit of family history." He grimaced. "Some would've trashed it. Aunt Alicia would've, for sure, if she'd found it. But why put it together with that animal paw? Those two things have nothing in common."

"Right, and what do they have to do with the hoard?"

Mark stood up and put the glass tube back in his pocket, under the slicker. "I'm flummoxed. Let's go." Linnet closed the umbrella and used it to help her get down from the crest of the whaleback without twisting an ankle. They had nearly reached the dripping eaves of the forest when Mark stopped short. "The hoard. That's the bit I can't swallow."

"You still think he was joking about that?"

"Yes and no. I think he was serious underneath. But, thing is, Lot never cared about money. He wouldn't have bothered to hoard it, even if he had anything more than jars of spare change."

"Then maybe he meant something else? What did he care about?"

Mark's gaze went inward, then he refocused on Linnet. "Know-ledge."

"What, just that?"

"*Just* the most important thing in the world, to Lot. He told me ignorance was our mortal enemy, and the war for truth was the only one worth fighting. He told me that more than once."

"He did say you were the only one who knew what really mattered to him. I guess that's why he left you this puzzle. This, what did he call it? A darkness that needs light shed on it?"

"Darkness is right! I don't even know what we're looking for!" He rubbed his forehead. "It's got to be dinnertime and I'm starving."

They plodded and squelched back down the slant of land. Mark was slower than he'd been on the way up, and kept hitting his head on low branches. On the brink of the last gully before the final downhill stretch to the gorge, he stopped short. "I've been thinking. Those two things, they do have something in common."

"Like?"

"Well, that paw is a righty, not a lefty, right?"

Linnet pictured it, and wrinkled her nose. "If you say so."

"And what happened after Violet's murder? A string of killings with the victims losing their right hands."

"But Violet's death didn't cause the killings!"

"We don't know, do we? Maybe it nudged some person who was just on the edge of going homicidally nuts. Maybe it was somebody close to her."

"Maybe. But why cut off the hands?"

"Another question. This story of what happened in 1892 is a mess of questions. And they never solved the murders, did they?"

"So that's the big mystery that Lot wants you to attack? The hoard of truth he wants you to find?"

"It's the best guess, isn't it? He's handed me a couple of pieces of a puzzle. There are a bunch of other pieces missing. For some reason he wants this puzzle solved. But why the hell didn't he tell me more?"

"Maybe he didn't know more. Maybe he only suspected. I bet if we knew who was that person he wanted you to speak to, we'd get more pieces. He also said to study the history of the site, right? Like, what happened here before 1892?"

"Good God in glory," Mark muttered. He slid into the gully and clambered out, talking in breathless chunks. "This sounds like— months of digging up—information! Years! He doesn't—want much—does he?" Then he stopped again, and took a couple of deep breaths. "*Didn't* want much. I keep forgetting he's dead."

"So what are you going to do?"

"Oh, solve the puzzle, of course." He caught his breath. "*And* catch the creeps who killed him. I owe him both those things."

They walked on down the hill. The long, squared shape of Lynx Leap showed through the trees ahead and below.

"I thought you'd given up on that. Catching creeps."

"Never. Only I can't do it by myself. Will you help?"

She laughed. "Just try and keep me away!"

Chapter 15

THEY PLANNED TO SPEND the next day, Monday, in the public library in the village, digging up history. Dell still refused to let anyone use the library in Lynx Leap. Mark suspected one of the keys he had found might fit the lock, but he hadn't yet had a chance to try it out, much less browse the books.

They got started on inventory duty early, to get it over with. Sorting and listing the contents of the one bathroom, the laundry, and the linen closet took them until eleven o'clock. When they came downstairs with their filled-out foolscap pads they found Jacob and Alicia with a visitor: a small, round man, bouncy with enthusiasm, who gaped in astonishment at the huge stone-floored entrance hall. He waved up at the dimly glinting chandelier. "I can just see this space with that thing all lit up!"

"And that's just the start," Alicia purred.

"We might have a buyer," Jacob murmured, as soon as Alicia had led the man out of earshot. "He's looking for an unusual site for an inn and restaurant. We're hoping he likes our views and atmosphere."

Mark grinned. "It's got atmosphere, all right. You can smell it!"

"Shh!"

"Sorry. But wouldn't it take a lot of money to fix the place up?"

"Not that much. The structure is as solid as a medieval fortress. Most of the changes would be cosmetic. Paint and a little replastering. The only thing that worries me is the cellar. Let's take a look."

As he spoke he led the way through the kitchen, grabbing a flashlight as he passed the refrigerator, and down the stairs. Mark and

Linnet followed.

"Good grief!" Jacob said, as he reached the bottom of the stairs. "I don't like the look of this."

He swept the long stone room with light. The floor was completely wet. New rivulets oozed down the landward wall.

Stooping to avoid the low beams, he splashed across to the room at the end of the cellar. Mark pointed out the crevice in the corner. Jacob poked his light into the crack and whistled. An echo fluted back at them, raising the fine hairs on the back of Linnet's neck.

"Sounds like it goes on for miles!" Jacob marvelled, still shining his light in.

"Dad, didn't you know about this?"

"Never saw it before. Never been down in this end of the cellar. Come to think of it, I believe there used to be a set of shelves in front of that door. Lot must have moved it."

"Or someone," Mark said under his breath, but Linnet heard.

They sloshed back across the main cellar floor. "Is it always so wet down here?" Linnet asked.

Every nerve in her body was alert to the floor's vibration and the dull boom of the gorge. She blinked away a mental image of giant hands beating a drum deep in the earth.

"No. Look there. That's new." Jacob's beam traced a crack down the landward wall from ceiling to floor. Water glazed it like a snail's track.

"But if the river is on that side...." Linnet looked over her shoulder, and back. "Where is the water coming from on this side?"

"Springs. Groundwater. Where most of the Lynx River comes from. The water table must be unusually high this year."

"The place is breaking up," Mark said.

Linnet backed toward the stairs. "Is it, Mr. Tanner?"

"Breaking up? Mark, don't be silly. The foundations are solid bedrock."

"The whole cliff's eroded, though," Mark said. "Lot said so, more than once. There's groundwater running all through the limestone, all along the Jaws. And with the heavy rain we've had, even bedrock isn't solid."

"Lot didn't know everything, Mark. He loved to be a doomsayer, he enjoyed getting under people's skin. I've got a geologist friend who might give an opinion, I'll get in touch with him. In the meantime, we need to get a padlock on the door in that partition."

"Already thought of that, Dad. I bought a lock yesterday."

"Did you!" Jacob gently punched his shoulder. "Good for you. Now you've got the job of installing it. Today. Okay?"

Mark nodded, but he looked glum.

VOICES SOUNDED in the entrance hall as they came upstairs again and started back along the corridor, with Jacob in the lead. "Good, the buyer's still here," he said. "That's encouraging!"

But the bouncy little man was not in sight. In the hall near the front door they found Alicia confronting a young woman in jeans and rain-spattered denim jacket. She was holding a heavy-looking leather briefcase open by one handle and fingering through the files in it with the other hand. "I know I brought it," she was saying.

"Jacob, this girl says Lot invited her." Alicia kept her cool eyes on the visitor's face, as if suspicious she might otherwise sneak off and steal something.

"Well, hello!" Jacob held a hand out, smiling. "I'm Jacob Tanner, Lot's grand-nephew. I'm glad to meet one of his friends."

The girl freed a hand to shake, pushed damp dark hair back from a round face and swept a smile around: at Mark, where he stood behind his father's elbow, and at Linnet beside Mark. "Not quite a friend, I can't claim that. More like a colleague. I hope he's well. He is here, isn't he?"

The silence that followed was the uneasy kind that means people are trying to think of how to phrase something. Her eyes flickered from face to face. "I'm Chantal Nadjiwan. I'm a doctoral candidate in Trent University's Indigenous Studies program. I have a letter of permission from Lot to pursue research on his land and in his house, if only I can find ... ah! Here it is."

She pulled out a folded paper, set the briefcase on the floor, unfolded the paper and handed it to Jacob. He read it carefully. "It's dated last month." He passed it to Alicia. "It gives Miss Nadjiwan permission to conduct investigations anywhere on Lot's property, and to see any artifacts. Also to search his library, and photograph documents."

"It's the library I'm especially interested in." She looked carefully from Alicia's face to Jacob's. This was not the welcome she'd been expecting, Linnet could see that. "I'm researching an encounter between the French and First Nations people that took place here in 1670. I believe there may be some primary materials here—journals, letters, that sort of thing—that may not exist anywhere else. Documents that could be extremely important to my thesis."

Alicia kept her eyes on Chantal's face. "You must not be aware that this house was built in 1851. There can't be anything to interest you here."

"With respect, I know the history of Lynx Leap." Chantal smiled, but her tone was suddenly crisp. "I know, for example, that originally most local papers of any historic value were kept in St. Mary's Catholic Church in the village. When the church burned down in 1860, they saved the archives and moved it to this house, since it was the

98

most substantial building besides the church. The storage was meant to be temporary, but even when the village library was built, in 1905, there was no other suitable place to store historical materials. So they stayed here."

"I'm impressed." Jacob looked staggered. "You know more about the history of this place than I do!"

"Thank you." She tipped her head at him, still cool. "Can you please tell me when Mr. Tanner will be back?"

"Oh dear," Jacob said. "I'm afraid—"

Alicia cut him off like a knife. "Lot is dead."

"Dead!"

"It was quite recent and sudden. So you see, you're in a house of mourning."

"I am so sorry." Chantal's hands rose, as if to touch someone, then dropped. "So sorry."

"And of course this letter of permission is no longer valid." Alicia refolded it and handed it back. "I'm afraid you've had your trip for nothing."

For the last minute Mark had been shifting from foot to foot and muttering under his breath. Now he bounced forward. "But that isn't right!"

"Mark!" Alicia snapped.

"It isn't! We should do what Lot wanted!"

"He has a point," Jacob said. "I'd be inclined to honour Lot's wishes."

Alicia gripped Jacob's arm with both her hands. "Over here." She steered him to the corridor leading to the study and stopped there, dropped his arm, faced him and hissed: "Are you insane? We can't allow a stranger free access to valuable papers and artifacts, especially that one. I wouldn't put it past her to steal whatever she thinks belongs to her people."

Linnet, standing in the centre of the hall, heard this clearly. So did Mark, judging by his reddening cheeks. *If we can hear it, so can she.* Chantal, when Linnet looked at her sideways, was gazing up at the chandelier as if this alone was what she had come to see.

"But this archives she mentions doesn't belong to us," Jacob said, not lowering his voice. "It's a public resource and we're just the custodians. And she's a qualified researcher. What right do we have to bar her?"

"May I suggest something?" Dell had come into the corridor from the library. "I agree with Uncle Jacob, she should be allowed free access. That's only proper."

Alicia opened her mouth. Dell held up a hand. "Mother, a moment? Here's my suggestion. We take inventory first and then we'll know exactly what's here. After that we can open the collection to serious researchers." She tipped her gleaming head at Chantal.

"Well!" Alicia tossed up her hands. "All right. Perhaps then. And by the way, I left Mr. Julien with you. Where is he?"

"In the study, looking at the built-in shelving."

"We'd better not leave him alone too long." They strode off together, heels clipping.

Jacob crossed the hall. Chantal dropped her gaze from the chandelier. He spread his hands apologetically. "We've decided."

"I know. I heard."

"Oh." Jacob thought back and reddened. "We, um, we'll definitely let you know when the archives becomes available. That's a promise. Do you have a card? Oh, good. Thanks."

"No, I thank you, Mr. Tanner." She slipped a card case back into her briefcase and snapped the lock. Then offered a hand. "You been very kind. And about the elder Mr. Tanner? I truly am sorry he's passed on. Not just because of my work. He was an unusual man and I wish I'd had time to know him better."

Jacob muscled open the heavy door for her, letting in a wave of wet air, and she was gone.

"Well, that was embarrassing," he said to the room at large, and hurried after Alicia and Dell.

Linnet looked at Mark. "I've thought of something. I didn't want to mention it in front of everybody else."

"Are we thinking the same thing? Lot's letter, the one on the memory stick?"

"Uh-huh."

"Come on!"

Chapter 16

CHANTAL WAS IN HER CAR, a mud-splashed green Elantra, and had just keyed the ignition. She rolled down the window when she saw them scurrying towards her through the rain. "Hi there!" She smiled at Mark, a flash of white teeth. "Thanks for speaking up for me."

Mark shrugged that off. "I was wondering if you could give us a lift to the village."

Her eyes, black and narrow and bright, flashed over both their faces. "Sure, hop in."

When the car was well started down the road, Mark, in the back seat with the briefcase and luggage, cleared his throat. "I'm Mark Tanner and that's Linnet Fox and I'm, um, ah, I'm sorry about my Aunt Alicia."

"Me too," said Linnet, in the front passenger seat.

"It's not important." Chantal flipped a hand on the steering wheel. "But I'm sad to hear old Mr. Tanner is gone. He seemed in such good health, really amazing for his age. Do you know what took him?" She clicked her tongue. "Listen to me! I'm a talker. If you'd rather not...."

"No, I want to talk about him," Mark said. "I believe he was murdered."

Her eyes darted to the rear-view mirror. Mark nodded firmly. The car jounced down the rutted road, sending water fountaining up from puddles on both sides. After navigating two more sharp bends she said, "You *believe* he was murdered. That means other people don't agree with you."

"That's right."

"Is there a story behind this?"

"Yes."

"A long one," Linnet put in.

"Well, I'd planned to drive right back to Trent." She turned the car onto the two-lane highway that became the main street of Lynx Delving. "But I'd like some lunch first. Anybody else hungry?"

BITING INTO THE GRILLED BLTs in the Pinetree Diner, sitting in a booth by a window, they had a chance to get a good look at Chantal Nadjiwan across the table. Mark stared shamelessly, and Linnet's discreet elbowing didn't inhibit him any. After wolfing down half his sandwich he wiped tomato juice off his chin and said: "Aunt Alicia thinks you're an Indian, but are you really? You could be part Chinese."

Linnet nearly choked. "Mark!"

"What?"

"How could you be so clueless? You don't say *Indian*! I mean, they didn't come from India. You say, um...." She looked at Chantal, who was watching them with a grave face and gleaming eyes. Was she angry? "Um, what do we call you?"

"Call me Chantal. It's my name."

"Uh ... but I meant...."

Chantal threw back her head and laughed. "I'm teasing!" She laughed some more and wiped her eyes with a paper napkin.

"But what *do* we call you?" Mark persisted.

"All right. You seem serious." She sipped coffee. "Linnet's right: 'Indian' is a misnomer. The preferred term is Native People, or First Nations, but that covers a lot of territory. Me, I'm Ojibwe. My an-

103

cestors, and others related to them, lived in Ontario for several thousand years before your ancestors arrived. But you didn't hitch a lift just to ask me that." She glanced around the crowded diner, then lowered her voice. "Why do you think Lot was murdered?"

Mark studied his hands, transparently sorting through what he knew or suspected and trying to figure out what to tell her. Linnet said, "It's because of his hoard, and the burglars."

Chantal sat back. "Hoard? Burglars?"

"That's what I said when he told me." Linnet took another bite of her BLT.

"The whole point is, there never was a hoard," Mark said. "At least, not of money." He told, without getting into fine detail, how the Tanner family fortune had become a local legend; how Lot, a bit of a miser, was believed to have amassed millions and hidden them in Lynx Leap; how he'd done nothing to squelch the rumours; how the mythical hoard had attracted thieves and vandals. "And then, about a week ago...." Mark took a deep breath and told how Lot had died, head-down on the cellar stairs.

Chantal was a good listener. She never looked bored or distracted, and she didn't interrupt. When Mark paused she said: "So you believe it wasn't an accident?"

"Yeah. The police think he just fell. My dad and the rest of my family bought that, but not me."

"Because of the robbers."

"Right. I found proof they'd been getting into the house through the cellar. I believe Lot heard them and went to check, and...." He spread both hands. "But that wasn't the end of it. Before he died, he left me a note on his computer, and it mentioned you, or I think it did."

Her eyebrows flicked up. "Couldn't you tell?"

"No, because he didn't finish the note. That was the day he died. Far as I can recall, this was what it said." Mark sat back, fixed his gaze out the window, and recited, with promptings from Linnet. "So you see," he finished, "if he wanted me to study the history of Lynx Leap, and he knew you were coming, and you're a history student, he must've meant I should talk to you." He looked at Chantal expectantly.

"That's quite a saga." She watched her hands cradling a coffee mug and thought it over. "But I don't quite see how picking my brain would help you any. I'm still searching for details on the 1670 encounter. I'm a long way from understanding exactly what happened then, much less why."

"You must know something," Linnet said.

"Oh, I know plenty!" Chantal flashed a smile. "And of course I know about the events of 1820 and 1892. Did you know they tried to pin the 1892 killings on the Ojibwe that lived around here?"

"That wasn't in the newspaper," Linnet put in.

"That's right, the local newspaper stuck to facts, so far as they were known. The big city papers didn't, though: they held a circus with this story. And of course there were hysterical rumours circulating, people claiming they'd heard drumbeats in the woods."

"Drumbeats?" Linnet's stomach flipped.

"From invisible drums." Chantal smiled crookedly. "There was also the fact that none of the victims were Ojibwe. But that was all they had to go on. So that line of investigation was dropped."

"You said 1820!" Mark leaned forward. "What happened then?"

"Something strangely similar. The 1892 massacre wasn't the first. It happened before, just about the time the British settlers started moving in." She sipped coffee and checked her watch. "I'll make it short. One settler built a sawmill on the gorge, as well as cabins for himself and his workers, on the site where Lynx Leap was later built. There was a quarrel over wages; the boss was accidentally killed; and then the culprits tried to cover up by murdering the boss's wife and young son."

Linnet pushed away the remaining half of her sandwich. But Mark was eager. "And then, don't tell me! There was a massacre, right?'

"Right. There were no police here at that time, so they sent soldiers up from the south. By the time they arrived it was all over. The men who did the original murder were among the victims."

"Did the Indians—sorry, Ojibwe—did they get blamed that time too?"

"No, because there were no native people in the region at that time. There hadn't been any since 1670. They'd all cleared out. And yet, funny how people's minds work, in 1820 there were still people who insisted they heard drumbeats in the woods around the gorge. The popular theory was that some wandering native had gone rogue and reverted to savagery. Only, no such person was ever found."

Linnet cleared her throat. "Did they have their hands?" It seemed important to know this.

"You mean, were the right hands cut off." Chantal studied Linnet's face. "That detail was recorded in military dispatches. Then in 1892, some reporter looked up the report on the 1820 incident and noticed the similarities. The mysterious drumbeats in the woods, the severing of right hands. And the numbers of victims. Both times, in 1820 and 1892, twelve people were killed by someone unknown."

Mark's eyes opened wide. "But how could that happen? Couldn't be the same guy, he'd have to be in his eighties, at least."

"The only credible explanation was that the 1892 massacre was a copycat crime," Chantal said. "Somebody knew all about the previous event and something inspired him or her to repeat history." She looked again at Linnet. "Are you all right?"

Linnet took a deep breath to steady her stomach and put on a smile. "Sure."

"This is horrific stuff. If you two have nightmares tonight, you can blame me."

"You'd know if it happened more than those two times, right?" Mark said. "I mean, something like that couldn't stay under the radar."

"Uh-uhn. Unless it happened in pre-radar days, so to speak. I have an idea, but it's too tentative to go into right now. That encounter in 1670 was not peaceful. Blood was shed." She turned up a palm. "But I don't suppose you're interested in my research."

"Sure we're interested!"

"Seriously?" She pretended to be astonished. "Okay, I'll send you a summary. Can I send it to Lot's email?"

"Um, better not. Lot's email is chancy now, with Dell all over the computer. But maybe you could send it to me at the *Leader* office. I'll just need a few minutes to fix it."

Chantal was ready to pay for their lunches, but Mark refused to allow it. "I can pay for mine and Linnet's. Lot says students never have enough money, and that's why he donates to scholarships." His smile faded. "I mean, he did."

"He was a good man," Chantal said.

Chapter 17

IT WAS STILL RAINING. Chantal got into her Elantra while Mark jogged to the newspaper office, a block away. Linnet waited in the back seat. Mark came back dripping and handed a scrap of damp paper through the car window. "I've got permission to use a spare computer at the *Leader* office. Here's the email address."

"Fine." She handed him a business card in exchange. Then beckoned. "Hop in a minute. Call me nosy, but I don't think you finished your saga about Mr. Tanner. Did you figure out what he meant by the rest of his message?"

"Well, yes." Mark got in, spattering water drops all over the dashboard. "It took us to the top floor of Lynx Leap." With Linnet's help, he told what they'd found there. Chantal's eyebrows were up for most of it.

"Quite a find. That letter of Violet Tanner doesn't change anything, but it does confirm guesses. I'd love to see a copy. But the other thing ... hm." Her eyebrows twitched down.

"I'll send you a photo," Mark said. "It's some animal's paw."

"Strange he would put those two things together." Chantal sucked her teeth, mulling it over. Then turned in her seat and scanned both their faces, lingering longest on Linnet's. "What kind of animal?"

"Can't tell," Mark said. "It's all dried up, it looks pretty weird. But it's got these big curving claws."

"Bear?"

"Don't think so."

"Linnet? What d'you think?"

Linnet couldn't speak. Thinking of the paw, with its claws poised to tear, made her feel sick.

"Well, feel free to get in touch. And be careful, will you?"

Linnet raised her head. "Careful about what?"

"Oh!" Chantal waved a hand and smiled, but it was a thin smile. "It's rough country up here. Don't fall down any potholes!"

THEY STOOD UNDER the window awning of the Pinetree Diner and watched her drive away. "So, our hunch about her was right. That was interesting." Mark stuck Chantal's card in a pocket. "Not sure how much use it was, though. Lot's mystery is still a mystery." He ducked his head against the rain and headed down Victoria Street towards the eastern end of town.

"It's even more of a mystery than before." Linnet hurried after him, warming her damp hands in her sweatshirt pockets. "It's like the same thing happened twice, 72 years apart. Why?"

"It's probably like Chantal said, a copycat killer."

"I can see that. But why that number twelve? And, you know what? It's got her worried."

"You think?"

"Yeah. Something in all that gave her something to think about, and they're not good thoughts."

Mark's plan had been to spend the afternoon in the village library, finding out everything they possibly could on local history. Somewhere, he argued, there had to be some fact that would fit into an empty space in Lot's puzzle, or at least give more shape to its darkness. But the library was only open on Wednesdays and Fridays in the summer.

"And we can't get at the library at home, thanks to Officer Dell."

He stood morosely in the rain, no longer even trying to stay dry. Linnet had her sweatshirt hood up and her shoulders hunched.

"Okay!" Mark straightened up and tossed back his mop of wet hair. "Change of program. Come on." He headed back towards the western end of town.

"Where are we going?"

"The OPP station. We're going to tackle your Aunt Theo again. I want her to tell me what Boyd Cray was doing every minute of the day Uncle Lot died. If there's a hole in his alibi—"

"You do that. I'm going back to the house."

"But—"

"I want a hot bath, if that's even possible at Lynx Leap, and I don't want to think about people getting killed!"

THE BATH WASN'T exactly hot, but Linnet came out of it feeling calmer as well as cleaner. Back in her room, dressed in fresh chinos and T-shirt, and with her hair blown to honey-brown silk, she was ready to check on the steel box.

Checking wasn't necessary: she had found what she hoped was a good hiding place for it, at the bottom of a carton of old books at the back of her closet. But the severed paw had been lurking in the back of her mind, not just in her closet, like a dark cloud on a sunny day. She wanted a good look at it by honest daylight, not that today's light was all that bright.

Carrying the steel box to her bed, she lifted out the leather bag and slid the paw onto the quilt. She was careful not to touch it with her bare hand. It looked like a scorpion, dangerous and alien, crawling on the clean white coverlet.

"What's it from?" she said aloud. "That's what gets me. I can't imagine what kind of animal it would belong to."

She also wondered who cut the paw from the animal, and when, and why. And how it got all dried out and mummified.

Maybe it was an Ojibwe relic: maybe they'd used it in some kind of ceremony. She wished she knew more about the people who had lived here all those thousands of years before the Europeans came.

There was no obvious segue to what she thought of next. A dark shape floated in her mind, a black leaf with glinting edges. The obsidian knife in Lot's study. Then she saw the connection. Paw, severed hand, knife. Linnet massaged her wrist. It was aching as if in sympathy.

What kind of animal? Maybe there was a way to find out. What clues were there? She bent over it and studied it closely, especially the claws, with their deep U-shaped hooks.

"Wicked! Some kind of predator, that's for sure."

She used yesterday's T-shirt to protect her hand as she picked the thing up and slipped it back into its bag. There was nothing rational about her physical loathing of the paw, but she didn't argue with herself over it. She couldn't stand to touch it, and that was that.

After putting the box back in its hiding place in her closet, she went downstairs to search Lot's study for answers.

She had the room to herself; just when she would have liked company. At hardly four o'clock, the thick cloud layer had pulled down an early twilight. The windows were blue, and they reverberated to the steady beat of the rain. When she flipped the light switch, a flickering yellow glow lit the room. The light steadied, but after that from time to time it dimmed.

Now, where to start? The study was like the library, the things on its shelves in no particular order, so far as she could tell. Maybe they were in an order that would have made sense to Lot, but he wasn't here to decode it.

After fifteen minutes of random poking along the littered shelves she found a book on the anatomy of mammals and set it on the central table beside the bear skeleton. The bear, she noticed, had long, heavy, smoothly curving claws, nothing like the hooks on the severed paw.

For 20 minutes the only sound in the room was the shaking and pattering of the windows and the rustle of turning pages. Linnet absently massaged her aching wrist as she studied the illustrations.

At last, with a frustrated growl, she slammed the book shut. Behind her, something jerked as if startled. She caught the moment out of the corner of her eye and twisted in her chair. Boyd Cray stood in the doorway. His face looked ill and bruised, the eyes sunk in dark hollows.

"You made me jump," he muttered. His left hand clutched his right wrist.

"Are you looking for Felix? He's not here."

"I ... no. I just wanted to see the place." His eyes darted like scared mice around the room.

"What's wrong with your wrist?" She asked suddenly. Her own wrist was sending shooting pains up her arm. Staring at him, she wondered: is this some kind of virus? Did I catch some horrible disease from him? She pushed back her chair and crossed the room towards him. Boyd backed into the corridor. She followed.

"Are you sick?" she persisted.

"No! I, I must've overused my wrist. You know, drumming. It's nothing." He turned and scuffed along the corridor to the front hall.

"Wait! There's something you want to tell, right?" She was only a few steps behind him when the lights flickered again and went out. A hush fell, a strange emptiness that struck her ear like a big, soft paw.

She looked around in alarm. Then realized what had happened. The unreliable generator had broken down. She had never been aware of its hum, because it was always there. But now it wasn't there.

Into the unfamiliar silence the sound of the river poured, louder than ever before, swollen by a day of rain. The spaces under the high ceiling amplified the sound to a booming, pulsing roar. Boyd let out a cry and pressed his hands over his ears.

Linnet lifted her head to listen. There was that drumbeat again, no longer deep in the earth. It was all around. Voices droned over her head.

Felix's mocking whisper came back to her. *The drums beat, and the shadows come creeping out of the woods.... That's when the killing starts.*

But Felix had been talking through his hat, as always. Mark was right, this was just a natural effect.

But why was it that Mark never heard the drumbeat? Why only her and Boyd? Because it was plain Boyd heard the drumbeat too, and it was shattering him.

"Stop it!" he screamed. "Stop it! Let me go!" He bolted for the front door, wrestled it open and was gone.

For a moment Linnet stood frozen. Then she ran out after him into the rainy dusk.

Chapter 18

"BOYD! WAIT!"

He didn't hear. Or if he heard, he didn't listen. He ran across the clearing in front of the house and blundered in among the trees. In a moment he was lost to sight, but Linnet could still hear the snapping and crashing of small branches tracing his path.

She hesitated. He was acting crazy. Maybe he was crazy. Who could tell what a crazy person would do next? Not only that, he was ten inches taller than she was and twice her weight, and if he turned ugly all the advantages would be his.

Odd, that she didn't feel afraid. She only felt sorry for him. Besides, she had to find out what he knew.

It took ten seconds to toss these thoughts around. Then she was across the clearing and crashing through the forest after him. She didn't waste her breath again shouting.

At this dark tag-end of afternoon, the woods were a blue tangle. The rain had slackened, leaving a million drops to trickle down through the layered leaves. A mist was rising from the soaked sponge of the forest floor. The birds were silent, except for an occasional dismal chirp.

After ten minutes of slipping and splashing, Linnet was out of breath, soaked to the knees and splattered all over with wet leaf-mould and mud. Her hair hung in dripping tendrils around her face. She would have given up and gone back, except that the crashing noises she followed were getting louder. She was gaining on Boyd.

Scrambling to the top of a steep bank, she saw him lying in a

114

heap at the bottom. Furrows in the soft ground showed where he had slid. She skidded down and landed on all fours beside him.

"Are you hurt?"

"Nah." He rolled over onto his back, arms spread out, head in the muddy leaves. "Tired."

"Okay, then! What's going on? What's this game you and Felix are playing?"

"Nothing to do with Felix. And it's no game." Water drops splashed on his face from the canopy above. He didn't move.

"Look, I won't get mad. I just need to know."

"You already know. You hear the same things I hear."

"What things?"

He moved his head irritably, making a squishing noise. "The drumbeats!"

"But.... I...."

"Don't lie!"

She sat back on her heels. "Okay. I hear them."

"Know what it means?"

"You tell me."

"It means we're chosen." The words were crazy, but he didn't sound demented. He spoke in a flat, dead voice, as if totally sure of what he was saying; and as if that knowledge had squeezed all hope out of him.

"What d'you mean, chosen? By who? For what?"

"Who?" He looked up into her face and showed his teeth in what might have been meant for a smile. "You've seen him. Don't pretend you haven't."

Ice touched Linnet's spine. She looked away.

"Thought so. Did he look at you? Did he catch your eyes?"

She hugged herself against a wave of cold. *Cat eyes in a human face.*

"I saw him five days ago," Boyd said, still in that dead voice. "It was just this kind of light. Twilight. I think that's his time. He was on the Leap, staring across the gorge at the house. Soon as I saw him, I knew. Knew I couldn't let him see me. If he saw me, that would be it. Finish."

"And then?"

"I guess he heard. Or just knew. He turned and looked at me. He saw me. I saw his eyes." He shut his eyes and drew a ragged breath.

"If I saw anything at all," she said firmly, "it was some poor homeless man. Probably the same man you saw. But he's gone now: he fell in the Jaws."

"The Jaws?" Boyd laughed. It was not a happy sound. "And they never found the body, right?"

He suddenly sat up and lurched to his feet, clots of mud dropping off him. Linnet jumped up and stepped back. He gaped around as if not sure how he'd arrived there. Then looked at Linnet. "You should go back wherever you came from. Get away while you can."

"Why me? Why don't you get away?"

"I've tried to leave and I can't." He started to turn away. She caught his sleeve.

"I don't get it."

"He won't let me. I tried twice. First time, I couldn't start my car. Second time, I couldn't get on the bus. Just couldn't. I'm stuck here now. Too late. Maybe it's too late for you, too."

He crashed away through the trees, not bothering to dodge low-hanging branches.

She watched him go and didn't try to call him back. *Chosen. Stuck here.* He was raving!

Better get back to the house. It was getting dark, and the mist was thickening. She climbed, using hands and feet, to the top of the bank, adding more mud to the coating on her hands, and looked in all directions. Now, which way? She hadn't the slightest idea.

Oh, wait. The river. Relief washed over her. Of course! Listen for the river. Steer for that sound.

But the sound of the gorge was a muted shushing, scattered by leaves and fog until it seemed to come from everywhere and nowhere.

All right then, Linnet told herself, go downhill. The river has to be down from here, right? Find the river's edge and follow it back to the house. Easy!

She started walking.

HALF AN HOUR LATER she admitted it. *I'm lost.* The chase after Boyd couldn't have carried her this far from the house. She might not even be heading in the right direction, might be wandering in circles like a nitwit in a cartoon.

Night turned the forest into a dream labyrinth, where she couldn't see more than two steps in any direction, and every shadow seemed alive. The mist formed low banks that drifted and eddied. Sometimes they billowed up into shapes like animals that slunk away and reappeared somewhere else.

In the fog, all sound was distorted. A loon's call quavered from what might have been miles away, or almost within reach. Every few minutes something small would rustle away through the undergrowth. Behind everything else flowed the endless, directionless *shush ... shush ...* of the river, never any closer or any farther away.

But as long as I can hear the river, I can't really be lost. All I have to do is watch for lights.

Twenty minutes later she was wondering if she'd have to spend the night in the woods. Maybe she should be looking for a dry place to shelter. If there was a dry place. Anywhere.

About then, she became aware that someone or something was following her.

The quiet, crunching sounds were not random. They had the rhythm of footsteps. She turned to face the woods behind her. "Boyd! Is that you?" But she already knew it wasn't Boyd. His footsteps would not be quiet, they would shuffle or crash.

"Felix! Can you hear me?"

Silence. The footsteps paused, then came on again, stealthy but not cautious. Not caring if she heard.

"Mark! Are you there? Answer me!"

Her throat dried up as she listened. Now the footsteps were very near. Small twigs crackled as they broke underfoot. Still there was nobody to see among the trees. Nothing but prowling fog shapes that could have been live things, or not.

What was it? Wolf? But they said wolves didn't attack humans. Bear? Only dangerous if you got in its way. Besides, it sounded like two feet. Human.

Whoever it is, if he won't answer, I'm not waiting around to say hi.

She turned and fumbled away from the sound. She walked almost blind, arms out in front to shield her face from the whipping branches. There was nothing to guide her, nothing to run towards. Only the noises behind to run from.

A fallen branch caught her across the ankle and sent her sprawling, hands squelching into mud up to the wrists. She scrambled up and stood motionless to listen.

The stealthy cracklings came more from the left, now. He—it— was circling, getting ready to come at her from the side. She turned to the right and plunged on.

Another sound swelled ahead of her. The river's mutter, now more of a growl. At last! Nearly there! Her stagger quickened to a run.

The foolishness of what she was doing didn't hit home until the ground vanished from under her feet.

Chapter 19

HER SCREAM CUT OFF as she landed sprawling. For a moment she lay with the breath squashed from her lungs. Then pushed herself painfully to a sitting position.

Thunder and the smell of water beat up at her from below. She was sitting, knees up and close to her chest, on a rock about.... She swept her hands out and back. About a metre deep and wide. Rock at her back. In front, below, was the river.

If I'd rolled when I landed, I wouldn't be here right now. I'd be down there. In the Jaws.

She flexed her shoulders, awkwardly stretched her legs, and took stock. Not as bad as she'd feared at first. Lucky to be alive! Bruised and scraped, but it felt like she'd get away without broken bones.

But what a place to be stuck in the dark! Linnet had the sudden notion that she'd been manoeuvred here. She'd been herded through the woods like a stray sheep. But what for? She elbowed the notion aside. "Get off your duff and get moving!" she snapped, in a fair imitation of Aunt Theo in short-temper mode. "Go! Now! Before it gets totally dark!"

She turned and groped up the back of the shelf, a steeply angled slope rough with jutting stones. Easy climbing, or would be in daylight. Even now it shouldn't be too hard to get back up to the top of the cliff, if she were very, very careful and took her time.

Another sound caught her ear. It came from the gorge. Something about it was odd enough to hold her there, listening. What was it? A gritty, irregular sound, something hard scraping on rock. You could

120

almost picture it: steel-toed boots, or a climber's cleats. No, there was no metal, it didn't ring. But somebody was down there, all right, and coming up.

Who would be nutty enough to go climbing up the side of the gorge, by choice, in the dark?

And then the thought came: *With the river roaring like that, if I can hear this guy that clearly, he must be close. Awfully close.*

Knowing she would never be able to turn her back and start up the slope with that unidentified climber within grabbing distance of her heels, she turned back, crawled to the edge and eased her head over to look down.

A face lifted to hers, the features invisible in shadow. The eyes two golden slivers, each bisected by a black vertical slit of pupil.

She knelt there, frozen. A scream built up in her throat. It broke free. She spun around and went up the bank like a squirrel.

"I'M TELLING YOU, it was a lynx!"

"And I'm telling you," Mark said, "it wasn't."

Moments after erupting from the gorge, Linnet had seen a flashlight beam swinging through the mist and heard Mark shouting. Now, after her second bath of the day and a bowl of hot chicken noodle soup, she almost felt human again.

They were in the parlour (which was what Lot had called it, not living room) and Mark had lit a fire in the fireplace. He built and nursed it as if he knew what he was doing. The furnace would not go on until October, he explained, at least that had been Lot's habit, but on cool summer evenings he often had a fire. The chimneys, unlike the generator, were in good working order.

The parlour was a long room off the north corridor. Everything here, as in the rest of the house, was dusty and shabby, but this had

121

been a showplace once. The walls were covered with ivory silk (Dell said) that still shone softly. Three elaborately patterned carpets overlapped across the stone floor.

Linnet, in pyjamas and dressing gown, curled up in one corner of the nearly napless plum velvet sofa, while Mark settled into the other end to read his camera manual. Dell sat in a matching plum velvet armchair reading a book titled *Oriental Carpets for Collectors*. From time to time she would look up and around as if pricing the pictures and lamps. Felix sprawled in front of the fire like a lazy cat.

All of them, even Felix, seemed content to be together by the fire, quiet and weirdly domestic. Outside, the river battered the foundations of the house and fog curdled at the windows, making shapes that caught the light like spying faces. Inside was a sense of safety as fragile as a wild bird's eggshell.

Linnet had decided that her forest stalker and her cliff-climber had to be the same, or at least the same species. "I saw the eyes," she said stubbornly, for at least the third time. "Those were cat's eyes. And lynx can climb, can't they?"

"They climb trees," Mark said. "I can't see a lynx climbing that cliff. He'd need pitons and a rope!"

Dell didn't look up from her book. "Lynx eat rabbits. Not people," she explained in a bored tone, as if to a four-year-old. "Besides, they're scarce in these parts now. I doubt there are any left."

"Maybe it was a cougar," Felix put in. "They're better rock-climbers than lynx and they've been known to carry off small children. A full-grown cougar would make two mouthfuls of a shrimpy little thing like Linnet."

Linnet tucked her dressing gown more snugly around her legs. "Shrimp? Speak for yourself!" Felix snickered and rolled over onto his back.

"You're way off, Fleabites." Mark prodded Felix in the side with his sneaker toe. "Cougars go after deer. And they're scarce around here now, too." He flicked a warning glance at Linnet, then added casually, "There's a stuffed cougar up in the attic. I don't recall ever seeing a lynx up there, though."

"There isn't one." Dell looked up from her book. "There's a space for it in Andrew's catalogue, but it's not filled in."

"There's a catalogue?" Linnet said. "Of stuffed animals?"

"Of the taxidermy, certainly. Andrew made the catalogue himself, leaving a space for *Lynx canadensis*. It was the only large animal he couldn't get."

"That must have driven old Andrew nuts!" Mark said. "Good for the lynx!"

"Don't joke. It's a valuable collection." She lowered her book and gave him a razor look. "And that, people, is why we want the items kept in good condition. People pay serious money for prime examples of taxidermy."

"And what does all this teach us?" Felix stretched. "If Linnet doesn't want to be tracked by curious cats, she shouldn't go wandering in the woods at night! Right, Linnet?"

Is that all that happened? she wondered. *Why do I still feel as if there's something tracking me, watching me? And if there's no stuffed lynx in the attic, what did I see up there last night?*

Lightning flared in her face. She blinked away after-images to see Mark fiddling with his camera. He flipped her a smile. "Testing!"

"You could have warned me!" She slid off the sofa. "I'm going to get a book." She left the parlour and turned toward the entrance hall. In the corridor she kept turning to look over her shoulder. She kept expecting to see Mark aiming his camera or Felix sneaking up behind, plotting mischief. The corridor was empty except for her, but it didn't feel empty.

The lights flickered again as she crossed the entrance hall. The voice of the river boomed and shushed out of the corners and down from the shadowy ceiling.

She climbed the stairs to her room. The walk along the corridor seemed longer than usual, the dimness deeper between the pools of light, the voice of the river more whispery and rhythmic. She marched along, back straight, refusing to scuttle, though she wanted to. She did not look back.

In her room she grabbed the book from her dresser and left again, walking briskly. The lights in the corridor dimmed to a bronze glow, then brightened again.

A faint sound behind. She looked back. Nothing. But her heart was beating at double time. *Pum-pom, pum-pom, pum-pom.* Still careful not to hurry, she started down the stairs.

She had just set foot on the landing, midway between the first and second floors, when darkness fell. The generator's hum died from the air.

Panic pounced. The book dropped from her hand and bumped and flapped down the stairs. She forced herself to stand still and breathe evenly. Exasperated voices sounded from the parlour.

You're okay, she told herself. Mark and the others were just over there. *Go on down. Hold the banister. Feel each step. Breathe.*

Linnet had taken only one step down when she knew she was not alone on the stairs. Someone stood close behind her. On the next step up, invisible in darkness. She could not move.

She took one breath, then another. She reached out and back. Her fingers met, not skin or cloth, but fur: deep and thick and coarse.

Chapter 20

AT THAT MOMENT the generator rattled into life. The lights went on. Linnet whirled around. The staircase was deserted except for herself. Nausea crept up inside. Again she reminded herself to breathe.

"Hold it!"

She twisted around again. Lightning dazzled her eyes. Mark stood at the bottom of the stairs, camera poised. She sat down suddenly and he let the camera swing on its strap. "Hey, are you all right?"

She crossed her arms over her stomach and gripped her upper arms, needing to hold tight to something.

"Linnet, what is it?" A touch on her arm.

She looked up to find Mark kneeling on the step below her. "Nothing."

"You look sick!"

She thought about telling him what she'd touched in the dark. Then took a look at his cheerful, skeptical face and decided to keep it to herself. "I'm fine. Thanks."

"Good." He looked over his shoulder, then back, and lowered his voice. "Still want to be included in any burglar trapping operations?"

"You mean for tonight? But didn't you put in that bolt in the cellar, like your father said?"

He waved a finger in the air. "Aha! I installed it as promised. But I *didn't slide it shut.*"

"So clever! That won't keep out any burglars, will it?"

"Well, no. That's the point. How can I catch them if they can't get in?"

She stood up, making a point of not hauling herself up by the banister, and collected the book from where it lay splayed at the bottom of the stairs.

"So? Are you in?"

"Mark, you're crazy. You're obsessed!"

"Just determined." His mouth flattened. "If you'd known Lot you'd understand. Yes or no?"

"Depends." She twitched a shoulder and shivered. "I wouldn't go up to the attic again at night, not for a million dollars."

"You won't have to. I plan to lie in wait by the cellar door in the kitchen. All you have to do is keep me company and make sure I don't fall asleep. And be a witness. There won't be any danger, I promise." He hefted his camera. "Soon as that flash goes off, they'll run like the rats they are."

"And if they don't run?"

"They will. I guarantee it. Be there at one o'clock."

LINNET TOLD HERSELF she'd agreed to Mark's crazy plan for his sake. If he was hell-bent on messing with prowlers, at least he shouldn't face them on his own. But the real reason, as she admitted to herself but not to him, was that after what she'd experienced on the stairs, she was afraid to be alone in her room. She needed his company more than he needed hers. Did he have any nerves at all?

She locked her door and closed the ink-blue drapes. The two halves of the window were still tied shut. She changed into jeans, light T-shirt, cotton sweater and thick socks. Then piled the pillows against the headboard of her bed and sat up, to keep herself from falling asleep. But sleep wasn't a threat. She tried to read, then decided that M.R. James's ghost stories were not the best thing to read when

126

you were all by yourself. She should have taken something less bone-chilling from the library when she had the chance.

She watched the clock. Just before one a.m. she tiptoed down-stairs, book in hand and flashlight sweeping the stairwell from top to bottom and side to side. She kept her imagination muzzled and blink-ered as she walked the length of the pitch-dark corridor to the kitchen, but there was no way to suppress it completely. Shadows wheeled away from her moving beam like giant wings. Her feet had an echo, a rustling patter as of running paws. She pushed these no-tions away and kept her eyes fixed on the yellow light that fanned from under the kitchen door, a beacon of safety in the darkness.

She found Mark spreading out a sleeping bag on the stone floor. A kerosene lantern stood on the table. Now that Linnet had arrived, he rolled down the wick so that the flame was a crescent the width of a nail paring.

"Might as well be comfy while I lie in wait," he murmured. He lay down on his stomach on top of the sleeping bag, facing the half-open cellar door. His camera sat on the floor in front of him. "You can sit there," he added, pointing at a hard wooden chair that stood between the sleeping bag and the table. "I brought cushions for it."

Linnet set sofa cushions on the seat of the chair and against its spindle back, and settled in. She reached out a foot and gently poked Mark in the ribs with a sock-covered toe. "You'll be snoring inside fifteen minutes."

"Not tonight, I'm jumpy as a cat. This'll be the night, I know it!" He pillowed his chin on his crossed arms and added, "Blow out the lamp, will you?"

Linnet hesitated, checked the dark corners, then leaned over and blew across the top of the glass chimney into her cupped hand. Dark-ness pounced. She immediately switched on her flashlight.

"No light!" Mark hissed.

She barred the light with her fingers. "I want to read! I won't sit here in the dark all night doing nothing!"

"You won't have to. I expect action in under an hour."

"Even an hour's too long." She opened the book and held the beam close to the page, keeping the circle of light as small as possible.

"Okay, but turn it off when I tell you," he growled.

After she had read most of the story called "The Diary of Mr. Poynter," Mark stirred. "Hey. Suppose you read to me."

"Starting to drift off?"

"Just read," he said grumpily. "But quietly! Whispers only!" He added, "What've you got?"

"It's the *Collected Ghost Stories* of M.R. James."

"Oh, ghost stories!" He hooted, but quietly.

"Mark. The story I've just finished, I promise you couldn't read it and laugh."

"Yeah? Give us a sample."

"Okay, here goes." She flipped pages. "'The sale-room of an old and famous firm of book auctioneers in London....'" Mark muttered "Bleh." Linnet breezed right over him. He was restless at first, shifting his legs, sighing ostentatiously. But as she slowly turned the pages he grew quiet. Finally he rolled onto his side so he could look at her, the better to listen.

When she reached the point where James Denton was feeling uneasy about the new curtains, with their pattern that resembled long, waving hair, and his sense that someone was peering at him through the strands, Mark suddenly raised his head. "What's that?"

He sat up and grabbed his camera. Linnet switched off her flashlight. For long moments the only noise was the faint gasp of stifled breathing and the pulse of the river, a sound so familiar now it was almost no sound at all.

"I was sure I heard someone on the cellar stairs," she whispered.

"False alarm." He lay down again. Linnet switched her light back on and sat cross-legged on the padded chair.

"Read some more," Mark said. "It was just getting good!"

"No." She closed the book, put it on the table, and muffled the flashlight against the front of her sweater. "Some things are better in daylight."

Mark pillowed his chin on his crossed forearms. "Well, you were right. I didn't laugh."

"Told you so."

"But, Linnet? Why do you read things that make you afraid?"

"I'm not afraid."

"You were scared reading that. Your voice went all funny."

"Okay. Maybe because I like to prove to myself I can be scared but it's not real, it's just a story. Don't you?"

"Nah. If I'm going to be afraid, it better be of something real."

"You have no imagination, that's your trouble."

"And you have too much."

She reached out with her toe and poked him again, not gently. "That's what my parents used to say. They wouldn't let me be afraid of anything. 'You mustn't be afraid of life,' that's what my father always says." She smiled at the shadowy wall. "When I was five he took away my night light. He said I had to learn there were no monsters in the closet."

"And did that work?"

"No. I just learned not to tell my parents anything. Especially not when I was afraid."

"Hmm." Mark turned on his side to look at her again. "Maybe

129

that explains your so-called lynx sighting. You imagined—"

"I did not!"

"Sh!"

They both held their breath. There was no sound in the kitchen but the ticking of the clock. Then Mark was up on his knees, camera in his hands. "Switch off!"

Darkness drowned them again. Linnet felt deaf and blind. Darkness filled her ears and weighed down her eyelids. There was only the dark, and the beat of the river, and the pulse of blood in her ears. Blood and the river: the same beat.

When the darkness took a shape, she couldn't move, couldn't make a sound.

It was so dark, it shouldn't have been possible to see the figure that stood in the cellar doorway. It was visible only because it was blacker than black, a hole in the heart of night. A figure shaped like a man, a tall man, only not quite. Not quite human.

Linnet couldn't move her mouth to shape words. Couldn't stir. Ice filled her veins.

It's a dream. A story. Wake up!

The blackness moved. Not walking or striding; it glided toward her from the doorway, with a stalking animal's fluid grace. Still no sound. Very near, now. Within arm's reach. She closed her eyes. It did no good, she still saw him.

A sliver of light came edge-on into the dark. It turned and became a leaf-shaped blade, bright with light reflected from some long-ago dawn.

Wake up!

The blackness moved. The blade rose, poised, swept downward. Terror burst inside Linnet and threw her screaming from the chair.

130

"I OUGHT TO TELL Uncle Jacob to send you home. Both of you."
Dell stood with hands on hips, gazing down in disgust at the mess on
the kitchen floor. "Honestly, you're such children!"

Nothing could ruffle Dell's icy calm, not even being shocked out
of bed at two a.m. by screaming and the crash of breaking glass.
She'd walked into the kitchen tying the sash of a blue satin robe
around her waist, not a hair out of place.

Felix was there too, craning over her shoulder. "What were you
two up to, anyway? Why the sleeping bag? Why the lamp?"

"I couldn't sleep. Linnet was keeping me company." Mark didn't
look up from where he knelt on the floor, brushing broken glass into
a dust pan. They had already mopped up most of the kerosene with
paper towels. The room still reeked with it.

"If that lamp had been lit," Dell began.

"But it wasn't, so no harm done. Doesn't anybody care that Linnet cut herself?"

"She'll live."

Linnet stood by the sink, rinsing antibacterial soap from the long
gash across the back of her right wrist. It was shallow, more scratch
than cut, but it had bled spectacularly. Crimson dots and dashes
spotted her white cotton sweater and spattered the stone floor.

Mark dumped the glass into a garbage can, then reached into a
cupboard over the refrigerator and pulled out a white metal box with
a red cross on the lid. Dell took it away from him. "Let me. You've
messed up enough for one night. How did it happen, anyway?"

"Linnet was reading to me and I guess we both drifted off. Then
she woke up suddenly and hit the lamp with her arm."

"You're very quiet, Linnet." Dell efficiently taped a sterile pad
over the cut and wound gauze around the wrist. "Is that what happened?"

131

"Yes. Sorry."

But it hadn't happened quite that way. Linnet wasn't going to tell anyone about the one skewed detail, a small matter of timing. The fact that the pain had flared in her wrist a full second *before* she struck the lamp and shattered the glass chimney.

Chapter 21

INSIDE THE HUT that called itself a bus terminal, the tall counter (chest-high on Linnet) took up half the space. It barely left room for one person on either side, and a public telephone bolted to the wall in one corner.

"I want to buy a ticket to Toronto, please. When does the next bus leave?" Linnet hoisted her backpack onto the counter, unzipped it and rummaged for her wallet.

"Tomorrow." The magenta-haired woman behind the counter studied the playing cards spread out in front of her.

"Tomorrow! But doesn't the bus go every day?"

"Sure does. Leaves at 8:55 a.m. You just missed it."

Linnet looked at the round analogue clock on the wall behind the woman's head. Its hands were at two minutes past nine. Missed the bus by seven minutes! "Augh!" She thumped the counter with both fists. "I can't stay here another day!"

"Sorry." A card snapped down, red jack on black queen. "Buy a ticket for tomorrow."

"Shoot! Guess I'll have to." Linnet groped uselessly in her pack again, then upended it on the counter. Playing cards went flying.

"Hey!"

"Can't find my wallet." She pawed through the clutter of small items, but the wallet wasn't there. She wouldn't be buying a ticket, not this morning. She rapped knuckles on her forehead. "How could I be so scatterbrained? I'm not like that!"

She'd slept perhaps two hours last night, if the fragments were added up, and fell out of bed that morning with her mind made up. She'd scribbled a note to Mark— "Thanks for everything, but I can't stay. Sorry!" —on a page from one of Dell's foolscap pads, and left it on her dresser. Spent 20 minutes washing, dressing, and packing, wasted no time on eating, left her suitcases to be sent after her, hoisted her backpack and headed down the road to Lynx Delving and immediate escape.

And forgot to bring money. Even if she'd been on time she wouldn't have got on that bus.

She looked over her shoulder at the public phone, an old rotary model with round slots for putting cash in. Fifty cents to place a call, a lot more for long distance, and she didn't even have a nickel. Lynx Leap, as she'd discovered, had no telephone. Lot had considered phone service too expensive. Here was the perfect example of how a cell phone of her own would have saved the day, if only her parents had listened to reason.

"You gonna clear that up?" The magenta-haired woman sat back, cold-eyed and indifferent. "I haven't got all day."

"Sure you have!" Then Linnet muttered an apology—this was nobody's fault but her own—swept the clutter into her pack, handed back a king and an ace, and stepped out into the sparkling morning air. A fresh west wind had blown away yesterday's rain and fog, but she noticed the improvement only with the edges of her attention. She was eaten up with the need to get away from this place.

Go to the police station, she advised herself. Borrow Aunt Theo's phone. Tell Mom and Dad to come and get me. Yes! Should've thought of that in the first place!

She started eagerly up the street. Then halted in front of the coffee shop and turned to confront her reflection in the window. "And explain, how?" she asked herself.

Go ahead, tell them the truth. Tell them a shadow tried to knife you last night. Tell them you're being stalked by an animal that disappears when the lights go on. Tell them you hear drumbeats when there's no drummer.

"Maybe they'll think I've lost my marbles. Had a breakdown. Wouldn't that bring them on the double?"

Her reflection rolled its eyes. *Dad will tell me to act my age, and Mom will tell me to find something better to do with my time than stage dramatics.*

She thought of telling Theo what had been happening at Lynx Leap over the last few days. She thought of begging to be allowed, at the very least, to camp out at Theo's place. She thought about it for only two seconds. Theo had enough to test her patience and, like Linnet's dad, once her mind was made up there was no way to change it short of dynamite.

"Linnet!"

She jumped and whipped around to see Felix crossing the street toward her. She expected he would make fun of her for talking to her reflection. Then saw he wasn't wearing his usual mocking half-smile. He looked unnatural without it, as if he was miming seriousness.

He reached the sidewalk with a jump. "Seen Boyd?"

"Yeah, yesterday afternoon. At the house, then in the woods."

"Woods? Boyd?" He sounded incredulous.

"What I said. He was upset about something. He ran off into the woods. I followed him but he...." Tell what Boyd had actually said? About the watcher, and the drumbeats? No. "He wasn't making a lot of sense."

"When was that?"

"Late afternoon, before supper."

"Huh. I wonder what's happened. You're the last person to see

135

him, far as I can make out. He hasn't been home." He turned and walked on, hands in jeans pockets, kicking at the pavement.

Linnet kept pace: not hard, with Felix's short stride. "Is that so strange for Boyd? Does he always come home when he's expected?"

"No. He sleeps out all the time. I don't think his folks care."

"So?"

"But he didn't turn up to play with Mister Styx last night. They were booked for a dance in the community centre, and he didn't show. Pretty much wrecked things for the band. That's what makes me think something's wrong. Boyd would never miss a gig. He lives for those drums!"

Linnet shot him a look of surprise. It sounded as if he was really worried about Boyd. As if he actually liked him. Maybe Mark was wrong: maybe Felix wasn't just using Boyd to annoy his mother.

"Tell Theo," she said. "Convince her to look around."

"Yeah, sure," Felix said morosely. "Like Sergeant Bloody Fox would ever listen to me."

"Hey, that's my Aunt Theo! She's not bloody, just a little, um, crusty."

"You say."

"Yeah, I do. And maybe she'll listen to me. Worth a try, right?"

As they walked towards the police station she thought of Boyd, crazed with fear, blundering through the woods in the dark and the fog. At least one thing he'd said had turned out to be less crazy than it first sounded.

I've tried to leave and I can't.

This morning Linnet had tried to leave. She'd bungled it so badly, there wouldn't be another chance until tomorrow. And who knew what might happen in the next 24 hours?

136

Chapter 22

LINNET RUBBED HER RIGHT wrist absently as she read. Under the gauze, the cut was still smarting.

"Linnet! Look up here."

She looked up, startled, to see Mark bending over the table and examining her forehead.

"Turn your head this way, more into the light. Oh boy. I was afraid of this." He clicked his tongue worriedly.

She let the book fall. "What are you talking about? What's wrong?"

"You've been stuck in here so long..." He rubbed a thumb over her forehead under the bangs, then opened his hand to show her a clump of vivid green. "You're growing moss!"

She laughed, and he dropped the worried look. "That's better. Look at the sunshine!" He waved at the window. "What have you dug up, after burying yourself in books for half the day?"

"Not much." She stretched her cramped arms above her head. "Just that the paw we found must have come from a cat. A big cat, I mean. It's got the right kind of claws. See?"

She turned one of the open textbooks in front of her to show him the illustration. He frowned at it. "But except for the claws," she went on, "that thing is nothing like any cat-type paw I can find!"

"Well, maybe it's not from around here at all. Maybe it's off some rare beast from darkest South America."

"I don't think so. Here's what the bones of a jaguar paw look like." She pulled another book on top of the first. "See? These bones are thicker and shorter than that thing in my closet. Besides, didn't Lot say the thing was found in the gorge?"

"What did you say yesterday about me being obsessed? C'mon, it's nice out. Come for a walk and let the wind blow away the cobwebs. Besides!" He gave Lot's computer a smack, making it wobble. "I've got stuff of my own to walk off. Or else next time I see Dell I might take a swat at her!"

"What now?" Linnet closed the books and stacked them neatly.

"She changed Lot's password!" He kicked the swivel chair and made it spin. "I can't use the computer! And now I can't download the last photos I took!"

"Oh no!"

"Oh, yes. And one of them, the one I took of you on the stairs, has something funny in it, but I can't make it out on the camera. I need to download it. Dell says," (He made his voice squeaky and finicky, not really much like Dell's.) "The computer might contain essential information on the contents of the house! It's not a toy!" He dropped his voice to a growl. "So that's what's bugging me, that and the fact that I haven't made a dint in Lot's mystery assignment. Now, what's eating you?"

"Nothing, really."

"Pull the other."

Linnet thought about that as they crossed the clearing and wandered into the wind-stirred, sun-dappled woods. How much to tell him? She liked Mark: liked him a lot. She didn't want him thinking she was weird.

"Boyd's still missing," she said finally. "Theo refuses to believe he's in any danger."

"I'd wait a few days before worrying about Boyd. Or a few weeks." Mark broke a leafy twig from a bush and used it to wave

138

away a cloud of tiny flies. The woods were full of them, this hot, steamy afternoon. "You've been wallowing in horror stories, Linnet. You're starting to imagine everything has a sinister meaning."

"A lot of things do. Look at the history of this place. What Chantal told us: about that murder in 1820. And then Violet in 1892. And all those other murders that came after."

"That was over and done with more than a century ago."

"Is it?" She ducked under a low branch.

"Yeah. Which is why I can't figure out why Lot thought all that stuff was important. Of course, if you're worried about those burglars, that makes sense: they're real."

"I'm not worried about burglars. I'm worried about something worse."

"Being stalked by lynx?" He made creeping motions with his hands.

"Mark." She stopped and waited for him to turn and face her. This wasn't easy. She had to take a couple of deep breaths before plunging in. He didn't make it hard: didn't poke questions at her, just stood and watched and waited. She was ready to unload everything. Then looked up and met his smiling, intelligent eyes in his sceptical, sensible face and decided: Some but not all. Not yet.

So she just told him about her feeling of being followed all yesterday evening. And the thing she'd touched on the stairs in the dark. His eyebrows went up as she talked.

"I was there when the lights went on," he said when she finished. "There was nobody and nothing on the stairs except you."

"Then what did I touch?"

"You probably brushed a hand against your own bathrobe. Remember that fuzzy thing you were wearing?"

"Mark, this was fur, not cotton chenille. I can tell the difference."

"I'm sure it felt like that. In the dark, when you're already nervous, it's easy to imagine things."

"Imagine, phooey! That's the kind of thing my parents would say!"

"And they'd be right." He started off again, breaking a path through the brush in front of her, waving the twig to ward off bugs. Over his shoulder he said, "I remember when I was small, I—"

The rest evaporated in a yell, and Mark vanished in a blur of flailing arms and wide-open mouth. There, and gone. As if the earth had opened a mouth and sucked him down.

"Mark!" She looked wildly around, then fell on her knees beside the place where he'd disappeared. Nothing was there but a dip in the ground, a bowl brimming with ferns.

Then the ferns thrashed and there was Mark's head, nestling among them. Linnet let out a yelp. *A severed head on a platter.*

"Well?" Mark frowned up at her. "I could use a little help."

With Linnet tugging under his arms, he crawled up out of the hole. He wiped mud and shreds of crushed greenery from his clothes. Linnet parted the ferns with the toe of her sneaker. "Is this one of those potholes you told me about?"

"Yeah, and I'm lucky I didn't break a leg! I think there's more to it, though. I couldn't see much, but there's a spot where it seems to go farther back. I think it could be the start of a tunnel." He did a little stomping dance. "This could be it!"

"You mean?"

"Yes! The unofficial back door to Lynx Leap!"

FIFTEEN MINUTES LATER they were back from the house with flashlights. Linnet had tied a scarf over her head. "There could be spiders," she said.

140

Mark lowered himself into the pothole. He paused, holding onto the rocky lip by his hands. "Once I'm down, you follow. "Go down backwards, like this." His head vanished beneath the veil of ferns and the last few words came up muffled.

As Linnet gingerly poked her feet into the hole, found rocky footholds with Mark's help and slithered down, she tried not to think of what else might be in there with her. She had a gut-deep aversion to things with more than four legs or less than two.

Landing with a squelch in mud, she turned on her flashlight. The pothole was a tall, narrow cave that smelled of wet earth and composting plants. The stony walls were green-mantled with moss, vines, and especially ferns, silky and feathery. Larger ferns grew near the mouth of the hole, screening it, as Mark had discovered. Daylight shining down through the screen made a glowing emerald patch high above.

Mark had already vanished among the ferns to one side. Then a light shone through, the ferns parted, and Mark's head stuck out all by itself again among the greenery.

"There's a tunnel here, all right. Come on!" He ducked back. Linnet pushed the ferns aside and squirmed after him. His voice bounced back at her from the irregular surfaces. "This is even better than I expected! Look at that! Bats!"

Linnet squeaked as something skittered past her ear. She remembered reading that you could catch a lung disease in bat caves. "Mark! Don't breathe in deeply!"

He was too fascinated to hear. "D'you see that? A white centipede! Look at the size of it!"

Linnet cringed. "Let's just get through, okay?"

The tunnel looked and smelled and sounded alien. Things grew here that she didn't want to touch: mosses and lichens so pale they looked bleached. Mark insisted on turning off the flashlights to see if the pale things glowed in the dark. For long minutes they stood in blackness that weighed like a mountain overhead, or an ocean.

Linnet's nightmare of two nights ago settled into her mind like an extra layer of darkness. The endless tunnels in her dream were like this. Only, in the dream there'd been something following her. Not now, of course.

She held her breath to listen. A breeze fanned her left cheek, bringing a whisper of sound.

"There!" Mark sounded awed. "Bizarre!"

Dim blotches were forming in the darkness. They looked as if someone had thrown phosphorescent paint at a black wall.

"Funny, what being in the dark does to your eyes," Linnet whispered. "I can't tell if they're yards away or only inches." She reached out cautiously and ran a fingertip up against one of the blotches. It felt like a scab on the tunnel wall. Lichen, maybe. "Inches."

The rock was vibrating beneath her fingers. "I can feel the river."

"We must be getting close to the house. Let's get going." He switched on his light and forged ahead, stooping under the jutting rocks of the ceiling.

"Wait! There's another crevice here. I wonder where it goes?"

"No side trips!" He suddenly sounded much farther away. He must have rounded a bend. *I ought to hurry and catch up.* But she stayed where she was, fascinated by the cool breeze that whispered in her ear. Her flashlight found a three-inch-wide crack in the tunnel wall.

Mark had talked of special effects, the other night up on the third floor of Lynx Leap. Here was another one: a sound like a chanted chorus, many voices twined together; but so faint and soft, they might be coming from light-years away. Or just years. She listened intently,

142

eyes closed. Hundreds of years.

She was almost sure there were words. Under her hand, the rock beat like a heart.

Linnet....

"Who are you?" she whispered. "Where are you?"

Then, from somewhere nearer, a cry of alarm, chopped off into silence.

Linnet snapped back to reality. "Mark! What happened?" He didn't answer. "Mark, are you all right?" Nothing. She headed along the tunnel as fast as she could go, tripping over rough places in the floor, squeezing through tight spots, ducking to avoid being brained by the rocky ceiling.

She manoeuvred sideways around a corner, dragged herself through a section like pincers and finally burst into a wider part of the tunnel. A lip of rock jutted up in front of her.

"Mark! Where are you?"

Still no answer. He must be hurt. Sudden fear sent her scrambling up the ridge and over.

Suddenly the ground tilted under her feet, and she was slithering and rolling down a slope smooth as polished marble. Her flashlight flew from her hand. The beam whirled like fireworks and then there was a crash and the light went out. Glass tinkled.

Linnet landed hard and lay winded, her head buzzing. When she sat up, she had lost all sense of direction.

"Mark! Are you here?" She held perfectly still to listen. No answer. Nothing moved. She was alone in the dark, except for the whispering breeze that had followed her. *Linnet ... Linnet....*

Terror dug its claws into her brain.

With arms clasped tight around her knees, she forced herself to think, to take stock of what lay around her. Panic retreated: not far, but far enough to let her mind work.

Something in the way her voice came back to her said that this space was bigger than the tunnel. Maybe it was a cave. Maybe a big one. There was water near: she caught a whiff of its cold, stony smell. Somewhere the gorge boomed, but in this absolute darkness she had no sense in what direction it lay.

A picture formed in her mind. The eroded cliff slowly crumbling. The rocks all around, just above her head, crushing downward, inward. *Don't think of that!*

All she had to do was get out and get help. It shouldn't be hard. Just go slow.

Rising cautiously to her feet, still crouching, she slid a foot forward. Her shoe met something soft, but resistant. Not rock or ferns, more like cloth.

She held her breath, bent and reached down. Yes, it was cloth. And there was ... something ... inside the cloth. It didn't move. She groped to the right, and felt hair. Hair and cold flesh. "Mark!"

Next moment her heart jumped, and she cried out again, as icy fingers closed over her wrist and gripped like death.

Chapter 23

SHE PULLED HER WRIST free and shrank away. Then reached out again. "Mark?"

"Yeah, me. Urgh."

"Are you hurt?"

He groaned. "Yeah ... no ... not much. Blacked out a minute. Hit my head."

The voice came from behind her, not from in front. Linnet froze, disoriented. "If you're there, then who's here?"

"Where?"

"Here."

"Hold on." A scuffling sound, then a clink of metal. "Found it. Wow, lucky!"

Light slapped Linnet in the eyes. She flung up a hand.

"Sorry." The beam moved down and lit the floor, ankle deep in grit and what Linnet hoped was not bat poop. Then it swung up and around. As she'd guessed, they were in a cave, but not a big one: really just a widening of the tunnel.

"Shine it over here."

The beam swung back and lit up a torn sneaker and a denim-covered leg. Mark sucked in his breath. He swept the beam to the face. He let the breath out. "It's Boyd. He's dead!"

"No. Look, he's breathing." The light showed Boyd's shirt rising and falling, just millimetres, but moving. He lay on his back, staring up at the ceiling with eyes that looked blind. Every few seconds the lids closed and opened again very slowly.

Linnet reached for his arm. "Boyd! Wake up!"

"Better not touch him." Mark moved the light back along Boyd's body. "He may have something broken."

"What happened to him?"

"I don't know. I think we'd better—" The beam stopped, spot-lighting a hand. The right hand. "Oh my God," Mark breathed.

No, not a hand. Just the place where the hand had been. What was left was a stump crusted with dirt and oozing blood, bones jag-ged white in the blackened flesh.

"WE'VE GOT TO GET help!" Mark stood up. "We'll get Dell to call Theo on her cell. I hope they can get a stretcher through the tunnel."

"Wait." Linnet had had a minute to think and she didn't like her thoughts, but they needed to be said. "One of us should stay with him."

"Why? He's not going anywhere."

"No, but I have this feeling. I mean, he's helpless. We can't go off and leave him alone."

"Well, okay. But we only have one flashlight. I'd better stay, the dark doesn't scare me." He made his face a grotesque comic mask above the light. "No imagination, eh?"

Linnet drew a shaky breath. She had already thought of this. "Just one problem. I'm, okay, admit it, I'm too short. I'd never climb out of that pothole on my own, without a rope or anything. But you could. You'll have to go."

Mark shone the light on her face. "You're sure?"

She smiled, she hoped convincingly. "Just go. Don't be long, okay?"

He studied her face a moment more, then swung the light away. "Okay. Back soon. Hold tight."

She watched him go, her sight of him obscured by drifting purple after-images. Watched the light die in the tunnel, and for what seemed long minutes listened to his bumpings and mutterings. Funny, how sound behaved down here, how one moment you couldn't hear anything and the next you could hear the smallest thing.

She moved a foot to locate Boyd, right in front of where she stood. Then used both feet to clear grit from a space on the rocky floor, shuffling and scraping for as long as she could make it last. Then sat down gingerly, pulled her bent knees to her chest, and made herself small and compact.

It wouldn't be long. Say it took Mark ten minutes to get to the house and get hold of Dell, then ten, maybe fifteen minutes for the police and paramedics to drive up to the house, then another ten for Mark to lead them back to the cave, he would be away for....

Wait. That was assuming there were paramedics in Lynx Delving. Maybe there weren't. But Theo would know what to do. So, say 35 minutes in all.

More than half an hour alone in here. Too long.

She sat in the dark turning her head, widening her eyes, trying to catch a gleam of light. But this was true dark. Not even the lichen patches with their ghostly white glow showed here. She shut her eyes and that made no difference at all. It was no darker than with her eyes open.

Maybe nothing lived down here, except bats, and if there were any right here they would all be sound asleep on the ceiling. Maybe there weren't any, which was fine with her. She'd hear something if there were bats up there above her head. Right? And there was nothing to hear, was there?

Just, somewhere, a faint trickle of water. And there were small stirrings all around, now that she listened hard. Little dry scratchings.

And something smelled bad. It wasn't a stink she knew, but it was unmistakably animal. Not human. It wasn't Boyd, for example.

Thoughtlessly putting her hand down on the surface beside her, she found gritty rock and something squirmed out from under her palm, and she shrieked and shot to her feet.

A picture formed in her mind: the rocks all around and above, crawling with....

"Stop that!" She crossed her arms and hugged herself. She could stay standing until Mark got back. Had to be ten minutes gone by now.

A scraping sound came from near her feet, and a mutter.

"Boyd?" She crouched, careful not to sit or put her hands down. "Boyd? It's me, Linnet."

Another mutter. It might have been "Help...."

"It's all right! Help is coming! Any minute now. We'll get you out!"

She listened, but there were no more mutters. "Boyd? I'm still here. You can't see me, but you're not alone." She talked to him, since he might be able to hear even if he couldn't talk, and it would comfort him. As it comforted her. Better than huddling silent in this nightmare place with her ears tuned for horrors.

"That's the worst, isn't it? Being alone. That's why I stayed, because I know, I can imagine how awful it must be. All alone in the dark, and hurt, and not knowing if anybody's missed you or anybody's coming to help. Not knowing if you'll ever see the sun again. But it's okay now. We'll have you out of here in no time!"

She paused to listen. He was breathing, she could hear it. That was the only clue he was alive. "I wonder how long you've been down here? Since I saw you in the woods last night? Let's see, it's oh, maybe two o'clock right now, so if you fell in yesterday around six, say, that would be, my gosh, 20 hours! But why couldn't you just walk out? Were you too hurt? You must've lost blood, maybe a lot. You could've been in shock."

Or crazy from fear. She knew, suddenly, that was what had done this to Boyd. Terror. The thing that had stalked her in the woods but not caught her, it had caught Boyd. It had done worse to him than cut off his hand.

He muttered. She bent over him. "Boyd? I'm still here. Can you hear me?"

"Linnet."

"Yes, it's me! Just hold on, Mark's gone to—"

"Told you." He sounded stronger. "Told you to get away."

"I tried."

"I can't stop it," he murmured.

"Stop what?"

"Can't end it. Now I'm punished."

"I don't understand."

She groped forward to find his sleeve. A hand grabbed her wrist and held on, surprisingly strong. She pulled away instinctively, then forced herself to relax. It was all right. He needed to hold onto somebody, that was all. So let him.

"Not much longer now," she said, although she had lost track of time and had no idea how much had passed. "Mark will be back, and my Aunt Theo. Soon. Any minute now."

Her knees were beginning to hurt: too long in the crouch. And Boyd's grip was tightening. Her hand was all pins and needles. "Um, Boyd? Could you not hold on so tight? Please?"

He said nothing, and she thought he had blacked out again. But his grip didn't loosen. Then his voice came clearly. "He's coming."

"Who? Who's coming?" He didn't answer. Maybe he meant

149

Mark. She strained her ears. At first she heard only the lub-dup of her own heart beating, it seemed, in her skull. Then that faded, or she filtered it out, and there was a different sound.

Voices, faint and far. Like what she'd heard at the crevice, but more distinct. A chorus: twined, layered. Sad voices. Singing, or so it sounded at first. But the longer they sang, the more it sounded like crying. Children crying.

Linnet's chest hurt. Salt tears ran into her mouth and dripped from her chin.

I can't bear it.

Silence. Then, soft, the drumbeat. *Pum-pom, pum-pom.* On and on. Drums in the dark.

Silence.

Footsteps.

"Mark?"

But she knew Mark's walk: brisk and confident, even in a place like this. Mark didn't prowl.

The footsteps padded nearer. Now there were eyes that gleamed opalescent. Cat's eyes. But not low to the ground like a cat. High up, like a man.

Linnet.

"No!"

She tried to stand, to back away, but Boyd still held her wrist in a grip like iron. She was trapped.

Chapter 24

"WE STILL DON'T KNOW who did it. Boyd refuses to talk." Theo swiveled her chair and moved her eyes around the semicircle of faces.

The sergeant's office in the Lynx Delving OPP station was uncomfortably crowded. It hadn't been built to seat seven people. And there were only four chairs. Jacob and Alicia sat in two of them, facing Theo across her steel desk.

Behind Theo, Kevin McKenzie rocked from heels to toes and back again as he ogled Dell, while trying to look as if he was gazing into space. Dell, cool and chic in a short white linen dress, her bare arms and legs tanned pale bronze, golden hair in a single perfect braid, stood behind her mother's chair and ignored Kevin.

Felix rated a chair between Alicia and Jacob. But it was no place of honour. He looked like a wilted dandelion, slumped with his yellow hair hanging in his eyes.

Linnet and Mark leaned side-by-side against the wall near the door. Linnet hadn't said much since the moment when Mark's distant shout had blown through the tunnel like a fresh breeze. At the police station she'd kept quiet and hoped not to be asked any questions.

"Refuses?" asked Jacob. "Or can't?"

"Refuses," Theo said. "He answers when he's offered food or pain killers. He's conscious, though he still seems in shock. The only injury is to his hand. He could talk if he wanted to."

Alicia shuddered delicately. "Who would do such a thing?"

"I can make a good guess. From what we know of his past crimi-

151

nal connections, I'd be willing to bet some unfinished business caught up with him. Somebody who wanted to teach him a lesson he'd never forget. Especially bearing in mind what Linnet reported."

Linnet shifted uneasily. She'd briefly told about seeing Boyd yesterday, but choosing what part of the truth to tell and what to leave out had been like walking through a meadow full of camouflaged potholes. Finally, all she'd been able to say was that Boyd had seemed upset, and there was a man he was afraid of, and he wanted to get away.

"But what about that hiker?" Mark spoke up beside her. "Remember? He lost a hand, just like Boyd."

"That doesn't have to mean the same person committed both offenses," Theo said impatiently. "What happened to the hiker got talked up locally and it put ideas in someone's head. We'll have to investigate, but I have no great hopes of nailing Boyd's attacker. Now." She pointed at Felix. "The immediate question is, what to do about this young idiot?"

Everyone looked at Felix. He sank lower in his chair. The last ounce of bravado had leaked out of him. Just one good thing had come out of today's horror: it had jolted a confession out of Felix. He and Boyd had been Mark's burglars.

"I could charge him with trespass and mischief," Theo said. "Also destruction of property. That stuffed deer was worth a fair bit. In my opinion, he deserves to be shaken up."

Felix sat up, white-faced under his blond mop. "But it was all just a game! A treasure hunt! We were looking for the hoard. If we'd found it, we would've given it back." He looked around at the ring of disbelieving faces and squeaked, "That's the truth! We didn't mean any harm, really!"

"What'd you do to Lot?" Mark came away from the wall, hands

clenched. "Did he catch you at it? Did he threaten to turn you in?"

"Lot? No!" Felix twisted around to face Mark. "He never—nothing ever happened. I don't know what happened to Lot. And neither does Boyd. I swear it!"

"Mark, back off. We're handling this." Jacob turned and gave him a quelling look and he subsided against the wall, muttering.

"Alicia?" Theo tapped a pencil on her desk. Her patience, always in short supply, was running out. "What's to be done?"

"Oh, do what you like." Alicia flipped a hand, bored and exasperated. Theo's gaze moved from mother to son and back again. As if reading judgment there Alicia added, "Since he got thrown out of school this last time.... That's what, four good schools that won't have him?"

"Five," Dell said.

"Yes. Since this fifth time, I've had enough. I honestly don't care."

Felix went even whiter than before. Jacob looked at him, then at Alicia. His mouth tightened.

"Well, you'd better start caring." Theo stood up and shuffled papers together, signalling they were done.

Alicia's chin went up. "I don't think you have the right to tell me how—"

"You'd better care, because I'm releasing him into your custody. From now on, you'll be held responsible for his behaviour."

"AT LEAST YOU CAN get some sleep now," Linnet said as she and Mark walked east along Victoria Street towards the offices of the *Lynx River Leader*. "You can call off the burglar hunt."

The sun, hot on their backs, was biting into the western ridge above the river valley. They had spent most of the last five hours

153

waiting around. Waiting at Lynx Delving's clinic, to find out what had happened to Boyd. Waiting until an ambulance arrived to transfer him to hospital in North Bay. Waiting at the doughnut shop for Jacob to gather the Tanner family. Waiting uncomfortably at the police station to tell Theo what little could be told about Boyd, and to see what would become of Felix.

Linnet felt wrung out, yet keyed up. She hadn't let herself think about what she'd heard and seen in the cave. *If I'd got on that bus this morning I wouldn't have to think about it. I'd be home now. I'd never have to think about any of it again.*

Yes, but it wouldn't be over. And Mark's still here and he doesn't know enough to be afraid.

"Call off the hunt?" Mark asked irritably. "How can I quit now? I still don't know who killed Lot."

"You're still sure he was murdered? Could Felix do that?"

"Well, no. I can't see Felix being that violent. Doing it on purpose. What's more, if he killed Lot by accident, I don't think he'd have the guts to keep it secret. I'm not so sure about Boyd. And Boyd has no alibi for the day Lot died, I've found out that, at least."

"Felix swears Boyd didn't do it."

"Uh-huh, and Felix doesn't have the sense he was born with. So who is he to judge?"

THE *LEADER* OFFICE was open late. "To be more accurate, it's open so long as I'm working," said Norris Urban, greeting Linnet for the second time in three days. "What can I do for you, chums?"

"I just came to check that computer for email," Mark said. "We're expecting messages."

"Okay, good. I'm working on the Boyd Cray story right now. Sergeant Fox told me just enough to whet my appetite, but I gather you two were right in the thick of it. So, before you leave here, let's have a chat."

AS THEY TRUDGED up the winding road to Lynx Leap in a deep blue dusk, horns beeped and blades of light swept around the bend behind them. They stepped to the side of the road to let a shiny black BMW pass. The car looked full of people. Behind it came a Jeep.

"There's Aunt Alicia! And Dad! What are they all doing up here?" Mark wondered aloud. "What's going on?"

He got his answer when they reached the house and found all the lights on. A thin, dark-haired woman in a tailored celery-green linen suit was striding from room to room, waving her hands, flanked by Alicia and Dell and trailed by a younger woman scribbling on a clipboard.

Jacob was standing in the entrance hall looking up at the chandelier. "That'll have to be cleaned and rewired," he said.

"Who is that woman, Dad? A buyer? I thought we already had one."

"No, the hotel man bowed out soon as he heard about Boyd. He said, what with Lot's death, and that hiker, and the rumours about thieves, there was already too much bad publicity. That woman is a decorator."

"You mean," Linnet said, "you're going to fix it up and live here yourself?"

Jacob laughed. "Never! We're determined to sell it. But as Alicia says, it'll take something spectacular to rescue the reputation of Lynx Leap. Which means no expense spared. And we've got to do it fast, because we can't afford to keep paying taxes on the place."

"I'M STARVING," Mark said, and headed to the kitchen, waving a roll of printed emails like a baton.

"I don't see how. You ate three crullers and a maple glazed at the doughnut shop."

"Doughnuts are mostly air."

"I'll be with you in two minutes." Linnet raced up the stairs to her room, changed into fresh chinos and T-shirt, brushed her hair, and was back down in five minutes. Mark didn't seem to feel the same need to shed the grime picked up in the course of their pothole adventure.

She found him standing at the kitchen table, busy with the ingredients of ham and cheese sandwiches. "Sit." He pointed the butter knife. "I'll make supper while you read."

Linnet sat down at the table and spread the curling papers out flat. Chantal's covering email was short. "She says she's attached a summary of events at Lynx Leap in 1670, so far as she has been able to determine by her own research and other people's. And she says we can ignore the little numbers scattered through the text, because they refer to sources, which would probably only bore us." She looked at Mark, who was slathering butter and mustard on kaiser rolls. "Sources? Oh, I get it. That's where she explains where the information came from. She's left off that part."

"Fine." Mark slapped together two sandwiches, cut them in halves, and poured two glasses of milk. "Let's have it. I hope it'll be some use to us."

"Okay." Linnet picked up two pages of closely printed text. She took a bite and chewed, while scanning the first page. "Hm. Fur traders and missionaries...."

"And Indians, oh my!" chirped a laughing voice. Felix popped his head around the doorframe.

"Scram, Fleabites." Mark twirled a finger, a signal. Linnet let the

156

pages roll up again.

"Whatcha got there?" Felix swung into the kitchen, hanging onto the doorframe like a pole dancer. "Share!"

Mark got up without another word, pulled a tarnished silver tray from a lower cupboard, loaded it with sandwiches and glasses of milk, and walked out of the kitchen. Linnet followed, the rolled pages in her fist. She met Felix's eyes as they passed and saw the laughter dying from his face. He didn't try to trail them.

Mark led the way to his room, where he locked the door and windows and pulled the drapes (his were yellow satin). He set the tray on the dresser, carried his milk and sandwich to the bed, and sat. "Where were we?"

Linnet sat cross-legged facing him, dropped the papers on the bed between them and started on her sandwich. "That was mean."

"He's a pest."

"I think he's lonely. His only friend around here is Boyd. Nobody else seems to like him, not even his own mother."

"He only has himself to blame."

"But you're his cousin. Don't you think.... I mean, now that he's come clean about the burglaries? He's like a balloon with all the air out."

"You feel sorry for him." Mark bit, chewed and swallowed the last of his sandwich. "I don't. Because I know him, and I don't trust him one inch. All that: 'So sorry, didn't mean any harm, would've given it back,' that's bullshit. And he's not looking for a friend, he just wants to find out what we're doing."

"I'm not so sure." She couldn't help feeling mean herself, and guilty. How different would Felix have been today if he'd found out at, say, age five how to make friends?

Still with glass of milk in hand, Mark picked up the pages and

157

ran his eyes over them. "Hey!" He opened his eyes wide at Linnet. "Another massacre!"

"Oh, no!"

"Oh yes! In 1670. Seems the one in 1820 wasn't the first. And look: here's this number twelve again. Twelve people with their right hands cut off! But wait, huh. This shaman. That's new. I wonder if that's where it started."

"Shaman? What shaman?"

He held out the pages. "Here. Read."

Linnet smoothed the pages and read aloud.

Chapter 25

THE FIRST FRENCH SETTLERS—or, to be more accurate, would-be settlers—on the site of what is now called Lynx Delving were a rarity. In 1670, almost all settlement in New France was along the St. Lawrence. The Ottawa-Mattawa river system was part of the trade route to Georgian Bay. While it was often travelled, there had yet been no settlement so far north.

The leader of the enterprise, Captain Etienne Dumas, had been an officer of the Regiment de Carignan-Salières. He, like others, was offered inducements to stay and settle in Canada when the regiment was dispersed in 1668. He gained permission to establish a settlement in the country north of the Mattawa. His idea was that the presence of a post on the Lynx River would induce more natives to come down from the north to trade their valuable furs. Dumas gathered 30 men, mostly ex-soldiers like himself, and travelled up the Ottawa River early in 1670. Their women and children were left in the south, to be sent for next year when a stockade and living quarters would have been built, and land cleared for planting crops.

A Jesuit priest, Fr. Henri Laplace, travelled with the company with the intention of doing missionary work among the natives. Following Jesuit custom, he had learned the Algonkin dialect, well enough to serve as interpreter. Most of what is known about the events that followed comes from Fr. Laplace's account, which can be found in *The Jesuit Relations and Allied Documents*.

159

The site chosen by Dumas for a settlement was hard by the Lynx River gorge, near the stretch of white water later named les Machoires (the Jaws). A band of 50 to 60 Algonkins, members of the Lynx Clan, lived here. The shaman (medicine man) of the band was its spokesman and appeared to be its most influential member. He refused to let the French settle by the river or cut trees there for a stockade. According to the Algonkins, this (like many other wild-water or waterfall sites) was sacred land, and under the protection of the clan totem.

The priest abhorred this reasoning as heathen nonsense. The totem lynx must be considered a demon. To assert the primacy of Christianity as a first step toward conversion, he held a ceremony of exorcism at the site described as being of greatest and most sacred power, a jutting rock above the wild water of the gorge that is today called the Leap, or Lynx Leap. The shaman, who claimed to be able to embody the clan totem, declared that the spirit lynx was enraged by the insult. If this injury was not avenged he would forsake the band, withdrawing his protection and guidance. There was only one way to fend off disaster without bloodshed, and that was for the settlers to decamp at once.

Rather than move on, Captain Dumas decided to teach the natives a lesson; and since the shaman seemed to be their leader, he singled him out to be the example. When the shaman came to the French camp, with two supporters, to negotiate terms, the French seized him, cut off his right hand, and cast it in the river. The two supporters were sent back to convey this warning but the shaman was held. The priest would have bound up his stump but the shaman refused.

Dumas, however, had misjudged the Algonkins. Rather than seek peace, that night the warriors of the band attacked the French. The war band included all males over the age of puberty, which was customary. It also included all adult women, which was so unusual that Fr. Laplace considered it worth special mention. Female warriors were rare among the First Nations of this region, then and later, although not unheard of. Accounts exist of individual Ojibwe women, for example, winning names for themselves in battle. But for all the adult women of the band to join the attack was extraordinary, and suggests that the aggravation (that is, the insult to their totem and the mutilation of their shaman) was equally extraordinary.

Dumas was aware that his men, 30 trained soldiers armed with muskets, could have caused great slaughter of these natives without risking serious casualties themselves. Wishing (to his credit, Laplace says) to prevent a massacre, as the warriors approached Dumas sent men secretly to the Algonkins' village, where only the children remained, supervised by a few girls in their early teens. These hostages were herded into a cave by the river, which opened into the gorge wall by way of a narrow passage. The shaman was forced in with them. A guard was set at the cave exit. The hostages were not otherwise harmed.

Dumas informed the warriors that their children and shaman would be safely returned when the natives had agreed to terms of peace, which included allowing the French to settle and freely build on their chosen site. What followed was the opposite of the intended effect, as the warriors attacked recklessly and would not retreat or submit, even when they were overwhelmed by French musket fire. When the battle was over all the warriors were dead: men, boys, and women. The bodies were counted: 43. They were

161

heaped up and burned.

All of this was recorded by the priest. He did not describe in detail what happened to the hostages, only noting what Captain Dumas told him: that they were gone and may have dispersed to allied bands in other areas. He also noted that, for a few weeks following the action, the region for many miles around seemed deserted.

Nearly a month passed. Then the company was attacked again. Within a week twelve French were killed, mostly individuals working or exploring in the forest or near the gorge. No attacker was ever seen; there was no enemy to engage. The surviving traders, still led by Dumas, abandoned the planned settlement and fled downriver, bringing news of the disaster to Montreal.

They also brought unsubstantiated stories, which circulated widely and were written down. A few said they had heard drumbeats in the unpeopled forest. Some said they had seen a ghostly white light in the gorge by night. There were rumours that the Devil himself, in the shape of a giant lynx, had been glimpsed prowling the stretch of the gorge now called the Jaws.

Fr. Laplace recorded all of the above but noted that he had no direct knowledge of the more lurid supposed happenings and had not himself seen the lights or heard the drumbeats. He suggested panic might have sparked these tales. But he noted as curious the confirmed fact that the settlers who were killed had all been mutilated in the same manner. In each case the right hand had been severed.

Chapter 26

LINNET TOSSED THE PAPERS aside and sat with her hands tight around her milk glass.

"Wow." Mark drained his glass and dropped it on the coverlet. "So maybe that's where it started. This shaman's hand getting cut off, and the warriors all getting massacred. But it doesn't shed much light on the mystery, does it? I mean, the numbers don't sync. There were 43 warriors, and there were 32 French available if you count Dumas and the priest. So if the French were killed as payback for the warriors, why stop at twelve? And why do it again 150 years later, and anyway who could.... Linnet?"

She uncurled her legs, slid off the bed and went and set her glass on the tray, not looking at him. "I'm tired. It's been a tough day. I'm going to bed now."

"Okay." He was watching her, head slightly tilted. "Comment?" He pointed at the papers.

"What's there to say? Forty-three people murdered. Muskets versus spears, or whatever they had. All of them, men and women and young boys. All killed and burned." Her throat was so tight it was hard to get the words out, but at least her voice didn't shake.

Mark was still watching her with that wary look. "I'm not sure it was murder. But it was bad."

"Bad. Yes. Do you have anything I can read?"

"Read?" He didn't usually sound stupid like this.

"Read. Like a book. I won't sleep tonight unless I have something to read." Something that wasn't ghost stories.

"No. I didn't bring anything."

"Not even a comic?"

"Sorry." He came off the bed. "Look, Linnet, if we could talk—"

"It won't help because it won't change anything." She turned to face him and stuck her hands in her pockets. "It isn't only that—that slaughter. It's the...." She paused to swallow saliva. It felt acid. "The lynx. The drumbeats. The lynx totem in that history, and what I saw in the gorge the other night, and, and what I saw and heard today. In the cave."

"The cave." He came forward, hands out. "You mean when you were in there with Boyd? And you imagined—"

"I didn't imagine!"

"Of course you did! Anybody would! Even I would, I admit it, alone in the dark except for a guy with his hand chopped off, I would've been seeing and hearing things." He dropped his hands and offered a smile. As if he'd cleared up the whole mess with this generous confession.

She walked out. No fuss, not another word, just went, and on into her own room, and closed and locked the door. She sat on the bed and tried not to think. A moment later came a bang on her door and Mark's voice.

"Linnet! We need to talk!" She didn't move. "Linnet!"

"Hey! What's all the racket?" A second voice: Felix.

"Get lost, Fleabites."

"You and Linnet have a fight? Lovers' quarrel?"

"Shut the hell up!" Another bang on the door. "Linnet!"

"Linnet!" Felix, laughing. Double bangs on the door.

"You two troglodytes!" A third voice: Dell's. "Get away from there and stop harassing that girl. And give me some peace!"

Mutterings, then silence.

164

After a few minutes of trying not to think, and failing, Linnet went to her closet and brought out a stack of the books she had unboxed to make a hiding place for the mummified paw. Almost all of them looked as deadly boring as they were dusty and smelly. An old Latin dictionary, a book called *The Republic of Plato* with yellowed pages falling out, an algebra textbook, a volume of Empire Club speeches. A few more like that. Amazing the stuff Lot could never throw away.

She put them all back except *The Republic of Plato*, flopped on the bed, and started in on it. "Hm. 'Some Current Views of Justice. The main question to be answered in the *Republic* is: What does Justice mean, and how can it be realized in human society?' Um, okay." If this wouldn't put her to sleep, nothing would.

She had doggedly worked her way to the bottom of the first page when there came a faint thump on her balcony. Then a tap on the window glass. She lowered the book and frowned at the closed drapes. Felix again! Well, he could just go back the way he came. She read on.

The taps continued, louder. She dropped the book and sat up. Better let him in, maybe. If he fell in the gorge on his way back it would be on her conscience. She crossed to the window and swept the drapes back.

A face pressed to the glass right in front of her. Not Felix. Mark. He straightened up, slipped the straps of a backpack off his shoulders, bent over it, and pulled out a box-like object about eight inches square. He held it up, smiling. It had knobs and a complicated-looking band of lines and numbers across its width and a steel rod that stuck out of the top at an angle.

It was a radio, although not much like the ones she was used to. Mark had risked his life jumping from his balcony to hers to bring her a radio, because he had no books to lend.

You are crazy, she mouthed at him, then got busy untying and unwrapping the linen sash from around the window handles.

"IT'S A TRANSISTOR RADIO." Mark set it on the dresser, switched it on and twiddled knobs. "I put in fresh batteries. Lot got it in 1964, he told me, and he never needed another. Still works real good. Hear that?"

"That" was a very loud used-car ad from Sudbury. He twiddled the knobs some more and found music, something very alternative and mournful; then a blast of oompah-pah, then a sweep of classical violins, then....

"I get it!" Linnet broke in. "Thanks!"

"You can get shortwave too. Comes in nice and clear, especially late at night. Once I got Moscow." He left the violins on, shifted his feet awkwardly for a moment, then strode in a determined manner toward the door. There he stopped, cleared his throat and began: "About that other thing. What you said about the cave."

"Not now, okay?"

"I know. I was going to say, I'm sorry."

"You don't have to."

"I do. That doesn't change what I think, but I wasn't laughing at you."

"Not much to talk about, have we?"

"Um." He turned the key, laid a hand on the doorknob, turned again and looked at her. "Linnet."

"Mm?"

"Your name, Linnet. I don't think I ever met another girl with that name. That's a kind of bird, right?"

"Yes, it's a variety of small, brown finch with a melodious song,

166

native to Europe and Asia."

"Sounds like you've said that a few times before. Suits you. I mean the name."

"My mother picked it because she liked the sound of it. I guess I should be glad she didn't like the sound of Flamingo. Or Cormorant."

"Or Blue-Footed Booby," Mark said, straight-faced.

"Or Yellow-Bellied Sapsucker." Linnet bit back a grin.

Mark snorted. "Or Western Tomtit."

"Careful!" She dissolved in giggles.

Mark wiped his eyes with his knuckles. "I'm going. Be sure and tie up your windows again."

"Thanks, Mr. Mom, I can look out for myself. But *you*." She stabbed a finger at him. "Next time you want to see me, knock on the door."

"I tried. Didn't work."

"After this I'll answer. Just promise me you'll never go that way again." She tilted her head at the window. "Okay?"

"Unless it's life or death."

LINNET WAS STILL SMILING as she closed the windows and tied the handles together with the linen sash. *Thanks, Mark.* She no longer felt as if she was standing on the edge of a cliff, fighting not to fall into the abyss. Might just get some sleep tonight after all.

She changed to pyjamas, turned out the overhead light and carried the radio to the bed. The station band glowed with a muted yellow light.

Bored with romantic violins, she played with the dials and knobs, no real clue what she was doing. Scraps of music and voices flashed out and away, as if the radio was a box crammed with jumbled sounds and she'd lifted the lid.

Then a man's voice spoke in a swift, liquid language full of curled consonants and throaty vowels. A moment of silence, then a woman singing: something mournful and longing yet not sad, rising and falling, now an arc of trembling notes, now a low dark sound like a river.

Linnet listened, spellbound. She wedged the radio between her pillow and the headboard, found the volume control after a couple of tries, and turned the sound down so it was just nuzzling her ear. The singer carried her away to a world far from this rocky gorge and dark forest. Her mind filled with sunlight, stones underfoot almost too hot to set foot on, brilliant white geometric shapes of houses printed on a sky of saturated blue. Slots of black shadow out of which people appeared and disappeared: men in fluttering white, women swathed in scarlet and parrot green and fiery orange. A soft warm wind that brought scents of roses and cloves and....

Later, she didn't recall dreaming. She woke at 3:25 a.m., according to her digital alarm clock. The radio was still on, its lighted dial spreading a glow on her pillow.

The singer was long silenced, of course. Static hissed and crackled. She reached to find the on/off switch and paused with her hand on the knob. Now there was sound, a distant sad song, a braiding of high voices in a minor key. Not something likely to cheer you, waking in the small hours.

But she kept listening. They were children's voices. They weren't singing, really; more like crying. *Oh, please. Not again.* Still she listened, as if this time she might understand.

Crying. Crying for help. Crying with fear. And whispering: calling, pleading. *Linnet. Linnet. Linnet.*

How do they know my name?

"Who are you?" she asked the darkness. "What do you want?"

168

Linnet. Linnet.

She clicked the radio off. The sounds faded slowly into the throbbing beat of the gorge.

What Boyd said in the cave. "I can't stop it. I am being punished."

Stop what? What did he know that he couldn't tell?

That something was going to happen.

Something was coming.

Chapter 27

OPERATION MAKEOVER, as Mark called it, got seriously under way early the next day, Wednesday. Alicia and Jacob arrived before the sun was up, followed by an army of plumbers, electricians, cleaners and painters. Vera Branagh, the decorator, seemed able to appear in three different places at any given time.

Over the next twelve hours, a new Lynx Leap began to surface from under the layers of dust, cobwebs and mildew laid down by decades of neglect. Woodwork and plank floors, sanded and refinished, emerged the colour of honey. Dark rooms grew bright and unexpectedly spacious. Walls glowed with delicate tints of cream and peach.

The chandelier was a major project. First it had to be unbolted from the ceiling and lowered to the floor. Then every single crystal was unhooked and carried to the kitchen to be carefully washed in soapy water, while electricians went into conference over the bronze skeleton.

Linnet offered to help, but was told by a coldly smiling Alicia to just stay out of the way of the workers, please. That would have been all right, except that Mark and Felix were no company. They were playing a ridiculous game of one-upmanship, with Mark mapping out strategies to lose Felix and Felix locating Mark by radar, or intuition. Wherever Mark and Linnet went—to the generator shed to check the coal burner; into the woods to search for lynx tracks or scat along the gorge—Felix turned up, strolling casually, happy to accidentally find his friends.

170

When they explored the tunnel in the woods, which came out into the cellar, as expected, Felix was waiting for them when they squeezed through the crevice. Mark returned his smirk, whispered "Distract him" in Linnet's ear, and sidled away. By the time she had detached herself from Felix and run up the stairs to the kitchen, Mark was nowhere to be seen.

In the corridor she was nearly knocked down by a new refrigerator travelling in on a dolly. She retreated up the stairs.

LINNET HAD RESCUED useful books from Lot's study and carried them to her room, which was to escape the full makeover. She went there now. As always, once inside the room, her eyes went first to the closet door. The mummified paw hidden there had a presence she could feel, as if it were alive and waiting for her.

Since Sunday morning, when they found the thing, she had brought it out two or three times each day and laid it on her bed and studied it. She always covered her hand with a sock or scarf to handle it. She still couldn't explain to herself why it repelled her, yet at the same time attracted her.

The thought came into her mind, idly at first and then insistently: There's something wrong with this thing. But what? None of Lot's books were any help.

Not until Wednesday afternoon.

Linnet was sitting on her bed, a book to the left and the paw, resting on its leather bag, to the right. She turned a page and looked. Then stared. Read the photo caption. A chill crept up her spine. She looked from the paw to the picture and back again. Shook her head. Couldn't be.

But there it was in black and white. She now knew what kind of animal had owned that paw.

PACK ON BACK, Linnet was halfway down the twisting road to Lynx Delving when she met Mark coming up. In one hand he carried a 9-by-12-inch manila envelope. "Hey!" He waved the envelope. "You're not leaving us?"

"No, I was looking for you. You weren't anywhere around, so I thought you might have gone to the village to get away from Felix. And bug Theo."

"Yeah. I did. Useless. But I got this—"

"Wait, I want to show you something." Linnet found a stump by the side of the road, an almost dry place to set her pack down. "You're going to argue, but this time I've got proof." She opened the top flap and pulled out a heavy book.

"Proof of what?"

"Proof that something's been happening here. Still is happening." She leafed through the pages. "Something ... evil."

"Evil" was not a word in Linnet's vocabulary. It was a word from old books, old times. But knowing what she knew, and what she feared, no other word seemed to fit. "Bad" missed the mark by a mile.

She looked up at Mark, expecting to see him grinning at her, but there was an unfamiliar shadow in his eyes.

"Me first." He opened the manila envelope and slid out a sheaf of pages printed with colour photos. "Got something to show you. Remember when I took your picture, Monday night? I downloaded the photos today at the *Leader* office. I can't explain this." He thumbed through the pages. "Bothers me."

She closed the book to take the page he held out. The printed photo, high resolution, about seven by ten inches, showed her standing on the stairs in her purple dressing gown, facing forward, left hand clutching the banister, right hand spread to the side as if to fend off something that stood behind her. Her eyes were two staring black dots in a white face.

Curling around her and rising behind her shoulder was a darkness that was not her own shadow.

"That shouldn't be there." Mark pointed with a fingertip, not touching the surface. "Your shadow is back *there*, clear as anything. So what's that?"

The photo trembled in Linnet's hand. Broken sunshine and leaf shadows flickered across it, making the details hard to see. She brought it close to her eyes.

"That" looked like a plume of dark smoke. Except it had shape: a sinuous shape that was not quite man-like, although the shoulders and head had a human outline. Its hand lay on the shoulder of Linnet's robe, and each smoky finger ended in a long, curved claw.

The sunlight grew stronger, washing the picture with light. But instead of growing more distinct, the shape began to fade. Then it was only a smudge. Then it was gone.

Linnet held a photo of herself standing on the stairs alone, white-faced and rigid.

Mark's lips moved, shaping words that never came out. He grabbed the photo and glared at it. Then looked at her with eyebrows knotted. "Did you see?"

"Yes."

Her legs felt like wet spaghetti. She sat down on the stump. That shadow-hand on her shoulder.... *It looked like it was tagging me. Choosing me for something. Boyd had used that word. We've been chosen, he'd said. Chosen for what?*

"I could've sworn...." Mark muttered. "But it must've been a problem with the printing. Hey, I'm sorry if I scared you for noth-

173

ing."

"Oh, no!" She bounced up. "You don't back out now. We both saw it, plain as day. There was something there with me!"

"Well, where is it now?"

"I don't know, but look at this." She picked up the book and opened it to a page marked by a strip of paper.

"Bones," Mark said. "Animal paws. A wolf, a lion, a chimpanzee, a ... hm."

"And a human hand for comparison, see?" Linnet reached into her pack and pulled out the leather pouch they'd found in the attic.

She opened the strings and slid the mummified object onto the book. It reached across both pages, digits spread, as if ready to rip and tear.

"I think I had an inkling almost at once. I just couldn't admit it to myself. But every time my own hand got anywhere near this thing, I got scared."

Mark's eyes went back and forth from the picture to the relic. "It's got to be a hoax."

"I don't think so."

"Dell was right, Lot had the scientific knowledge to manufacture a thing like this."

"How?"

"Easy." He picked it up and brought the curved claws so close to his eyes, Linnet grew cold inside. "You take the bones of a human hand, and you glue on the claws of a big cat—a lynx or cougar—and then you cover it with skin. And...."

He dried up. His eyes moved from the claws to the joints, examining every millimetre, top and bottom. "Man! It sure looks like the thing actually grew like this."

Linnet let out the breath she'd been holding. She held out the pouch and Mark slipped the hand back into it. Pouch and book went into her pack. Mark stuffed his photos back into the envelope.

"Okay, something's going on," he said as they trudged up the steep road. "Or did, years ago. We know that. All those coincidences, the massacres, the severed hands."

"Yeah, like Boyd. And me." She massaged her right wrist. Under the healed scratch, the ache was bone-deep.

Mark aimed a fingertip. "That not better yet?"

"Oh, it's fine." Then she kicked a rock up the road. "No, it's not fine. I think I just missed ending up like Boyd, that night in the kitchen."

"Don't get carried away, you still have your hand." He was growly. Maybe that was the way worry took him. He added: "We've got about a hundred questions without answers. Some of our facts look pretty damn weird. Hard to explain. But that doesn't mean we go all Twilight Zone, okay?"

"All right, never mind, then."

"That photo, for example, you saw how the sun took that smear right out."

"It wasn't a smear! It was a shape."

"Of what? No, it was a flaw, probably a leak from the ink cartridge. And that thing?" He rapped his fingertips on the backpack, with the book and the paw in it. "That can't be what it looks like."

"Mark!" She dug in her heels and yanked his arm to make him stop and turn around. "Can't you believe your own eyes? Lot wouldn't give you something that was a lie, would he?"

"No, I don't think he would. But one thing I do know: Lot knew about animal anatomy. He'd been collecting specimens all his life. He knew, for sure, exactly what that is. And he knew for sure there's no such thing as a human-lynx hybrid."

175

"But—"

"So it has to be something else. Maybe it is a lie and he wanted the truth about it to come out. Maybe that's the mystery he wants me to solve."

They walked on in silence. Linnet said nothing more about the paw or the photo. She hadn't been thinking hybrid, anyway. She'd been thinking of a sentence in Chantal Nadjiwan's research summary. "The shaman, who claimed to be able to embody the clan totem...."

But Mark would never accept that, or whatever it implied. It wouldn't fit his view of the world. The more weirdness they discovered, the more stubbornly he hung onto his belief that everything would make sense in the end. And the more Linnet became convinced that none of this would ever make a daylight kind of sense. This darkness was too old and too strong.

They walked up the road side by side, but every step took them further apart. She had made a friend, and now she was losing him.

Chapter 28

IN THE HOUSE they split up. Mark muttered something about *hungry* and headed towards the kitchen. Linnet climbed to her room to empty the backpack and hide the mummified paw (no, the hand) in her closet again, although she began to think there was no point. Who would want to steal it? What did it mean to anybody but her?

Restless, she wandered downstairs again. It was close to six o'clock, but the electricians were still crawling around the dismantled chandelier. Sounds of electric sanders and polishers came from the study and the parlour. The kitchen was the one quiet room on the ground floor: the crystal washers had finished and gone, and the gleaming new appliances were installed.

Mark was sitting at the maple slab table spooning up canned beef-and-rice soup, with a plate of sliced and buttered bread alongside. When he saw her he got up, went to the new stove and filled a second bowl, and set it on the table across from him. "Eat up!"

"Thanks." She sat down and dug in. "This stove works, does it?"

His brown eyes smiled at her. "Like a charm. Lot wouldn't know the kitchen now. Or the rest of the house either. He'd hate it!"

So they were still on speaking terms. She wouldn't lose her new friend. That is, she wouldn't so long as she stuck to safe topics.

"Oh, and here." He reached around and pulled a folded paper from his back jeans pocket. He tossed it on the table. "When I was at the *Leader* office printing those photos, I checked for email and there was this from Chantal."

Linnet picked it up, unfolded it and scanned it silently, while

177

continuing to spoon up soup.

Greetings, fellow researchers! Today, on a Catholic historical data website, I found an itemized index to the St. Mary's archive: the collection now held in the Lynx Leap library. One entry mentions a letter from Captain Dumas to his son.

It's a long shot, but I'm hoping this is the piece that will help me fill a serious gap. I wonder: is there any way you can get to see it? If you can persuade Dell to let you find and scan that item, I will be in your debt, and hers. The file number is 1717.

But this is a lot to ask: so if it's impossible or too much bother, don't worry. I will wait patiently until Mr. Tanner tells me the collection is open to researchers. Chantal.

Linnet laid the paper aside, away from soup splashes. "What d'you think?"

"About persuading Dell? Not a chance. Once her mind is made up it's like surgical steel."

"That's too bad. Specially since that thing Chantal wants, that letter, might help us solve Lot's mystery, too."

"Or at least shine another ray of light. But not to worry!" He winked.

"Hm?"

He set down his spoon, dug in a front pocket of his jeans (good thing he wore baggy jeans, because his pockets were always crammed, Linnet thought) and tossed a small jingling heap on the table. She poked them with a finger.

"These are the keys we found Monday."

"And I've been trying them out, whenever the coast was clear.

They're all working keys and one of them opens the library."

"Hoo boy, wait till Dell hears that!" A new voice, but familiar.

Linnet looked up, startled. Mark dropped his head into his hands and growled like a dog. Then raised his head and swivelled to face Felix, who stood draped against the doorframe. "This has nothing to do with Lot's nonexistent hoard, Fleabites! It's about history. Nothing to interest you."

"I know what it is." Felix peeled away from the doorframe and sauntered into the room. "It's you and Linnet in cahoots with that Indian woman who wants to get her hands on our stuff."

"It's not our stuff. It's a public resource. Dad said so."

"Besides," Linnet put in, "she's okay about waiting for it."

"But you're not, are you, Moron?" Felix punched Mark on the shoulder. "And you've got keys. Alicia will just love that."

Mark scooped up the keys and stuffed them back in his jeans. "Now you're calling your mother by her first name?"

"Well, you heard what she said yesterday. I'm not going to call her *Mom*." Something flashed in his face. Linnet held his eyes; then he looked away.

Mark said: "So, why d'you want to give her any satisfaction?"

Felix pulled out a chair, sat down, put his elbows on the table and smiled from Linnet's face to Mark's. "I don't. But I will if I don't get what I want."

"And what's that, Fleabites?"

"Stop calling me Fleabites!"

It was the first flare of honest anger Linnet had heard from him. "He has a point."

Mark sniffed. "Is that all?"

"No. I want in on your action."

Mark sat back and laughed. "Action! There is no action! I keep

179

telling you!"

"I don't mean the hoard. I just want to be part of whatever you're doing. I've been watching you and something's up, I know it." He folded his arms. "You push me off, I go straight to Alicia."

Mark raised eyebrows (Now what do we do?) at Linnet, who shrugged (No idea). Then he looked at Felix. "How do we know you won't spill your guts anyway? You never could keep a secret."

"But I will this time because I'll be in on it." He sat forward eagerly. "You see? If I'm in it with you, I can't drop you in the poop without getting myself in too! And just to prove how useful I can be, here's something." He sat back again and smiled, catlike. "I have inside information. You want to search the library and not get caught? I know the perfect time."

ALL THAT DAY, with the comings and goings, the hubbub of voices, the whine of floor polishers, the clatter of ladders, Linnet barely heard the voice of the gorge. But that night, after the workers left and Jacob and Alicia drove back to Lynx Delving, the house fell silent. And the pulsing beat of the river rose again.

Linnet turned on the transistor radio and kept it on until she was starting to drift, then switched it off. No sad choirs this time. But there were dreams. Twice, she woke gasping from a vision of running in panic through dark tunnels.

The third time she woke, she was standing at her window, tearing at the sash that bound the handles as if her life and sanity depended on getting that window open. As if something horrible was crawling across the floor towards her.

She took a flying leap back into bed. Tomorrow morning she would get some heavy twine from the kitchen, or better yet, some wire, and rewrap the handles, double- and triple-knotting the cord.

Make it so nobody would ever untie it, especially not herself.

After that she lay awake wondering. Had Felix been innocent that other time, Sunday, when she'd wakened in the small hours and found her window open and river water on the carpet? And what would have happened this time if she'd gotten the window open without waking up? Where would she be now?

OPERATION MAKEOVER continued on Thursday. The elegant but shabby old furniture was cleaned and repaired, at least where it would show. Tattered carpets were rolled out and fresh new ones rolled in. Dusty drapes came down and airy curtains went up. The electricians performed surgery on the skeleton of the chandelier.

Even Lot's study was overhauled. Now it looked like a museum, with carefully chosen specimens arranged behind glass, shelves and tables polished, and the computer moved to a corner. A telephone was installed there for the first time in the history of the house, with an extension in the kitchen.

The bright weather continued as well, but tricklings from the creeks and streams and the sodden forest fed the already swollen river. Jacob made frequent visits to the cellar and came up looking worried. "Two new cracks," he told Alicia in an undertone.

At noon he drove to Lynx Delving to confer with real estate agents and lawyers, and to have invitations specially delivered to everyone who was anyone within a 20-mile radius. Lynx Leap's rebirth was to be celebrated with a reception on Friday evening.

At one o'clock, just as Felix had said, Dell and Alicia set off for North Bay to meet the caterer. They would be gone for six hours.

Chapter 29

THE HOUSE WAS STILL full of people, but none of them cared what a trio of teens were up to. Mark unlocked the library door, held it wide and waved Linnet in with a sweep of his other arm. "Six hours? Plenty," he said. "With any luck we could be out of here in fifteen minutes. Or less."

Linnet still felt half-guilty about what they were doing, although they had talked it out yesterday evening. Mark had no qualms, or so he said. "Aunt Alicia's attitude is plain wrong. And Dell's just being a pain in the butt. As if Chantal would steal anything! And my dad, he only gave in because he knew Alicia would make his life hell if he didn't. Dad's a totally nice guy, but the flip side is he's too easy to push around. I'm not."

Once inside the library with the door closed, Linnet looked around and wondered if even six hours would be enough. It was not a small room, and it was just as full of books as it had been the last (and only other) time she'd seen it.

There were differences. It was cleaner and tidier. The windows had been scrubbed, letting in more daylight, and hung with cream linen curtains. The books all stood in rows on shelves, all their spines lined up like soldiers. The ones that had been stacked in corners and on windowsills and crammed in on top of others had been fitted in where they belonged, or moved somewhere else.

Linnet looked around doubtfully. "Mark? Where would the archives be?"

"No clue."

She gaped at him. "But you've been coming here how many years? How could you not know?"

He turned up his hands. "I hardly ever came in the library. I was usually outside."

"Felix?"

Felix was at the central table, head down on its newly waxed surface, chin on crossed arms. "Why would I ever come in here? Dead boring place."

"Incredible. Don't you two ever read?" She looked around again and brightened. "Well, Dell's got everything organized and labelled. That should help."

Dell had taped cards on the ends of the shelves, neatly lettered with labels such as BIRDS, REPTILES, MAMMALS, INSECTS, GEOLOGY, FOSSILS, CLIMATE, ECOLOGY, LOCAL HISTORY, and FIRST NATIONS.

"There's eight whole shelves of local history," Linnet said. "Some of this has to be the archives. Let's go through it." No action from the two boys. Felix sprawled on the table, bored and listless. Mark was frowning back and forth across the room and up at the ceiling, then gazing blankly into space.

"Guys?"

Still looking distracted, Mark joined her and together they ran fingertips along the spines of books, reading titles, Linnet starting at the left ends of the shelves and Mark at the right, and meeting in the middle. Felix got up and wandered around nervously, finally fetching up at one of the windows, where he twitched aside a curtain and looked out at the sunny clearing and the woods.

They had finished the fifth shelf from the top and were about to start on the sixth when Felix turned around and said: "Isn't archives supposed to be about papers and letters and stuff? Not printed

183

books."

Linnet's hand fell. She scanned the bottom shelves and saw nothing that looked like papers, or files, or whatever might be used to hold them. Nothing but books.

"I have a bad feeling." She walked along the shelves. Books, nothing but books.

"Maybe this archives is kept somewhere else," Felix said. "Up in the attic, could be."

"But it's supposed to be in the library! Chantal said so!"

"Lot could've moved it." Felix pushed away from the window and stretched. "To make room for his own stuff."

That was so possible, even likely, that Linnet slumped into a chair. "Then we'll never find it. We might as well email Chantal and tell her it's no go. Mark? What do you.... Mark?"

Mark was stiffly pacing the length of the room, parallel to the corridor, like a toy soldier wound up and set going. He reached the south end of the room and muttered, "Eight and a bit. Plus eight inches for the depth of the shelf."

He about-faced, caught Linnet's eye, flashed a wink at her, and walked out the door. She followed. In the corridor he was doing the same thing. Starting from the library doorway, he paced stiffly and deliberately south, stopping with his nose against a narrow door at the end of the corridor. He turned around. "Eureka!"

"Because?"

"Something's missing."

"Wait." She was getting a glimmer. "Are you saying...."

"Yep." He scudded back into the library, sweeping her ahead of him, and closed the door. Then beamed around as if he'd just won the Nobel Prize for Physics. "Something about this room was bothering me and I couldn't figure out what. Then it hit me. It's too short! So I

184

paced it. Counted my steps."

"How very scientific," Felix muttered. He turned his back and stuck his face through the gap in the curtain.

Mark pulled a pencil and a small spiral-bound notebook from a pocket and scribbled. "The study and the library are the last two rooms at this end of the house, one each side of the corridor, right? There's nothing else at this end. Except the generator shed, and that's outside, past the end wall. Okay." He pointed the pencil at the library door. "From there to the south end of this room is about 20 feet. But if you go out and pace from the doorway to the south end of the corridor, it's 26 feet. They should be the same and they aren't."

The south wall of the library looked like all the other walls, solid with shelving and books. No door. "So there should be another room there," Linnet said. "Where is it?"

"Dunno. Hidden. Not much of a room, only six feet deep."

"My gosh. I wonder if—Felix?"

He'd reared back from the window. Now he spun around. "Car!"

"But," Linnet began.

Mark was moving. Felix was already out the door. Linnet followed, stopped in the doorway to look back and make sure nobody had left anything behind or messed anything up, then stepped out. Mark closed the door and locked it. "Scatter!" he hissed, and headed across to the study.

Linnet was halfway along the north corridor to the kitchen when she heard the front door grate open and, a moment later, Felix's surprised-sounding voice. "Dell! Thought you'd gone to North Bay!"

"Mother did. She rented a car. I just went into the village to talk to our local suppliers. Why? What mayhem did I interrupt?"

"Nothing much. I found your secret chocolate stash."

"Fool. You know I don't touch the stuff."

185

"I'M NOT TOTALLY convinced. He could have known." Mark kicked stones down the road. They were walking, not anywhere in particular, just away from listening ears.

"You don't think maybe you're just a tiny bit paranoid?" Linnet intercepted a stone and kicked it onward. "He did give the warning before she could catch us."

"He could've been playing with us. Let us *almost* get caught. That would be like him."

"I think he was playing fair. He's lonely, he just wants to be part of it. Give him a little credit."

Mark gave in grudgingly, after more argument. "Tonight when Dell's asleep, we'll do it. I'll watch the light under her door. You put out your light and wait till you hear me tap. Then no talking and we shield the flashlights until we get downstairs."

LINNET WAS DOZING when the tap came on her door. It was 2:12 a.m. In the corridor she made out two dim shapes, and followed them. The boom of the gorge swelled and echoed as they felt their way down the stairs. It sounded as if the river was flowing fuller and higher, if that was possible.

Once in the library, Felix uncovered his flashlight. "About time! I thought you'd dumped me."

"Careful! Keep the lights away from the windows. Dell could still be awake and she could see our lights if she looks out. I thought she was planning to stay up all night!"

"Doing what?" Linnet asked.

"Something on her computer. Tap tap tap, on and on, like a robot."

"I have often thought Dell must have been stolen as a child and returned as a cyborg," Felix said. "Now what?"

Mark led the way to the south end of the room. He pulled books from the shelves at random and poked a hand through, then pulled it back, shaking his wrist. "Ouch! Solid wood back there. I was hoping we might see through."

"We could take out all the books and then move the shelves." Linnet tugged at one side of a shelving unit. "But if it's nailed to the wall.... Oh."

The three-foot-wide bank of shelving, heavy with the weight of books, was suddenly floating in her hand. One side had swung forward like a door. Linnet let go and backed away. The three of them stared at the inch-wide gap. Then Mark bent down and slid fingers under the bottom shelf. He straightened up. "It's on wheels!"

"This is so cool it's giving me chills," Felix murmured. Then he spun to face the others, face alight. "Hey! This is it!"

"What?" Mark said, then waved a hand. "No."

"Yes! This is where he stashed the hoard! Why else a secret door?"

"Well, let's see." Mark pulled on the shelving unit and it swung all the way open, the wheels smooth and almost silent. Behind they found a door in a recess: a normal one made of dark panelled wood with a brass knob, a match for the library's main door. Mark grasped the knob and turned. It wasn't locked.

The space beyond was small and dark and smelled of paper, and it hummed. There were no windows. Three flashlight beams ran over industrial-style metal shelving filled with beige cardboard cartons, some flat and some deep.

Mark stuck his head in, than reached up the wall. An overhead light went on. Lower down beside the door, a small box-like machine hummed and breathed cool air up at their faces. "Look, a dehumidi-

187

fier."

Felix ran his light back and forth, searching. "I don't get it. What is all this junk?"

Mark laughed. "Good old Lot. I guess it was his hoard, sort of."

"It's the archives," Linnet said.

"Right, and Lot was in charge of it, while it was here at Lynx Leap. You see what care he took of it. Shut out the light, controlled the moisture. He took his job seriously."

"But why hide it away like this? Why keep it secret?" Linnet asked.

"I don't think he did. You saw how easy it was for us to find it."

"Then why not just leave the regular door showing? Why the shelves on wheels?"

"My guess?" Mark was still smiling. "He just didn't want to give up any shelf space. If he'd done that, he might've had to get rid of some of his books!"

"What a total crock." Felix kicked the doorframe. "I bet Dell found this and didn't even think to mention it." He turned away. "I'm going back to bed."

Mark looked after him and nudged Linnet. "Hurry!"

It didn't take long to find what they were looking for. The cartons were all numbered; the numbers looked like dates. "They're grouped by year." She ran a fingertip along a shelf. "See? Here's three boxes with stuff for the year 1825, and the next one is 1826—two boxes—and on like that."

"I hope 1717 wasn't a multi-box year." He knelt to search a lower shelf. And it wasn't. He stood up holding a flat box; held it out; Linnet opened the lid and lifted out a single manila folder. She looked in again. "This is all there is."

"Good." He put the box back in its place. "Now we disappear."

188

Two minutes later they stood in the corridor. Mark locked the library door. Then he darted across the corridor into the study, and a moment later was back. "It's hid," he whispered. "Also the keys. Just in case Fleabites decides to pull the plug on us. If I'm searched they won't find anything incriminating."

But there was no stern-faced Dell waiting on the stairs. Felix had played fair.

Chapter 30

"I HAVEN'T HAD a complete night's sleep since I got here," Linnet complained to the back of Mark's windbreaker as he tramped up the path ahead of her. "A full week!"

"I wanted to get out of the house before Felix changed his mind about keeping secrets."

It was six o'clock Friday morning. The eastern sky behind them was a sheet of rose-gold shining through the trees, the western sky ahead still purple with earth-shadow. The dawn air bit cold through Linnet's sweater. Not what she'd expected in not quite mid-August. "When does winter start in these parts, Labour Day?"

"You'll feel better once you get your blood whipped up. Here we are."

They came out from under the eave of the woods as the sky brightened, scrambled up the crowning ridge, and scaled the granite whaleback. Linnet turned to face east. The sun had climbed up with them and flashed into their eyes. The clouds caught fire: scarlet, crimson, magenta, all the reds Linnet could name, and more she had no names for.

"Red sky in the morning, sailors take warning." She squinted under her hand.

"Lucky we're not sailors." Mark sat down on the curve of stone and opened the canvas tote bag he'd carried looped over his shoulder. The only thing in it was a large manila envelope. Inside the envelope was a 9-by-12 light beige cardboard folder, the one they'd taken from the archives. Inside the folder was a cardboard envelope. Inside the cardboard envelope was a large sheet of tissue paper folded over. Inside the tissue paper was a single heavy sheet of blotched, yellowed paper closely covered with brownish handwriting.

"My gosh," Mark said. "I'm afraid even to breathe on it."

"Better try not to. That file number on the box, 1717, that must be when this was written. Captain Dumas to his son, didn't Chantal say that? A letter nearly 300 years old!"

Mark bent over it, then sat back. "It's in French!"

"Well, yeah."

"My French sucks. How's yours?"

"Not bad."

"Okay, you read it." Gingerly, holding the letter by its edges inside a frame of tissue paper, he moved it from his knees to hers.

"Okay. Um...." This would not be easy, even though she'd always been good at French. The handwriting was one barrier: it was full of little curls and hooks, and some of the S characters, she realized after some puzzlement, looked like small Fs; and the writing was wobbly and uneven, as if the writer had been old or weak or sick, or maybe all three.

"Here's something else." Mark fished a page with typing on it from the file folder. He passed it over. It said: *The enclosed letter was written by Captain Etienne Dumas to his son Alain Dumas, Montreal, May 3, 1717. Dumas the elder died later that year at the age of 82. The letter was kept by the family and consigned to the care of the archivist at St. Mary's Catholic Church, Lynx Delving, in 1848.*

"Huh, a letter written the year he died," Mark said. "Any bets it's just a bunch of good advice and who gets the best furniture?"

"I don't think so. I can sort of make out bits. It starts 'Mon cher fils,' My dear son, and then it says, 'Ceci c'est une....' I think...." She raised her head. "It's a confession."

191

Mark thumped his knees. "Now we're getting somewhere!"

"Maybe not very fast. I think a lot of French words were spelled differently 300 years ago. I can't make out much. Wait, here's 'enfants,' children, and here's ... yes ... 'Algonkin'! And something ... could be 'vengeance,' but...." She set the letter down and folded the tissue over it.

"No good?"

"It's impossible! Even if I could read it all, I couldn't be sure I'd got it right."

"Never mind. We'll get it to Chantal." Mark carefully repackaged the letter and stowed it in the canvas tote, then stood up. "I wonder what he was confessing."

Linnet wondered the same thing. She didn't like some of the ideas that came snaking up from the depths of her imagination.

Shoving the snakes back down, she turned in a circle, taking in the immense swath of forest from one horizon to another, wave beyond wave of green lit gold by the rising sun. Mist drifted up from the Lynx River gorge, caught the sunlight, glistened, and faded. Far to the west, on the skyline, lay a long, bumpy band of dark purple.

"What's that?" She pointed. "Those hills. What are they?"

Mark looked. "No hills. That's cloud. Coming this way, probably. Better enjoy this nice weather while it lasts."

AN HOUR LATER they were eating fried eggs, bacon and hash browns in the Pinetree Diner. Half an hour after that they were in a second-floor windowless cubby of the *Lynx River Leader* office, scanning the letter and sending it to Chantal Nadjiwan as an email attachment.

To make sure she read it right away, Mark got permission to use the office phone to call Chantal in Peterborough, at the number printed on her business card. He had to leave a message, and delivered it glaring at the wall and stammering. "Um, hi. This is Mark. Tanner. Mark and Linnet, you remember? We found that thing you're after, uh, file 1717. But we can't read it. I just emailed it to you, I mean a scan of it, and if you could let us know what it says, that would be really great. Um, Linnet? Anything else? No, okay. Then I guess, um, thanks, 'bye for now."

He clapped the phone down and looked at Norris Urban. "Thanks for this, I owe you. I'll pay for the call."

"Forget it!" Norris waved that away. "Yes, you do owe me, but you can work it off the summer you're sixteen. As an unpaid intern. We'll work on your telephone skills."

AT NINE O'CLOCK they were back at Lynx Leap. Mark had decided the best thing to do with file 1717 was to hide it in his bedroom until the next time Dell was busy somewhere else, then get it back where it belonged PDQ, "as Lot used to say." He had printed a copy of the scan so they could study it; they didn't need the original.

The front door had just closed behind them when a car door slammed outside. A moment later Sergeant Theo Fox strode in. She gave Linnet a nod but no smile. "Mark! Where's your father?"

"Don't know, I just got here myself. Why?"

"Boyd Cray walked out of North Bay Hospital two hours ago. Any sign of him around here?"

"No." Mark frowned. "How could he just walk out?"

"He may be missing a hand, but he's got the use of his legs. And anyway they couldn't stop him: he's not under arrest. Yet."

"Yet?" Linnet echoed.

"He stole a car near the hospital. Stupidly, right under a security camera. Nobody seems to know where he is now. Or care."

"He could be anywhere," Mark said.

"But he wouldn't come back here," Linnet put in. "He wanted to get *away* from Lynx Delving."

"I hope he does," Theo said. "He hasn't been good for it and it hasn't been good for him."

Linnet realized that under her grim crust, Theo was one who cared. "If we see him, what should we do?"

"Call me. They did put a phone in here, didn't they?"

"Sure," Mark said. "But what're you afraid of? Boyd can't do much harm to anybody now."

"He can harm himself. Tell your father." She turned away. Then turned back, pulled a folded newspaper from her belt and tossed it to Mark. "And tell your friend Norris, his lead story's already out of date."

It was the Friday issue of the *Leader*. The page one headline read: LYNX LEAP BREAK-INS SOLVED, SUSPECT FOUND MAIMED.

"SO THIS IS D-DAY." Mark grinned at Linnet over a basin of soap-suds. "Delusion Day."

"Shouldn't it be P-for-Party day?" She polished a last bit of tarnish off a silver salt shaker, then slid it into the basin.

He dug his hands into the suds. "No, D. Because it's all about creating a delusion that Lynx Leap is a house that anybody might want to live in, so they'll buy it and take it off our hands."

"But Lot lived here, how many years?"

"Nearly a hundred. But he lived hard: harder than people want to these days. I visited him once or twice at Christmas and the place was a refrigerator. He didn't mind, just wore lots of sweaters."

Operation Makeover was winding up. Trucks rumbled up the

194

road to widen, flatten and gravel the clearing, suitable for parking. Window washers lowered a scaffold from the roof to clean the glass on the river side of the house.

The caterers arrived and took over the kitchen, dining room, and study. Linnet and Mark were assigned to clean silver and glassware, carrying basins of water to a flat rock at the edge of the new parking lot to do the job. Dell collected the cleaned sparklers and arrayed them dazzlingly on sideboards and in display cabinets.

Once finished the polishing, Mark was detailed to help set up a corner for the musicians in the entrance hall. Linnet was roped in to serve as general helper to the caterers.

Felix had evaporated, which meant more chores for everyone else, but Linnet was glad to have lots to do. While rolling carts of glasses to the dining room, where the bar was to be, and setting out elaborately folded linen napkins on a long table in the study, where Alicia wanted the buffet to be, she had less time and head space to think about those four words she'd been able to decipher in Captain Dumas' letter.

They still surfaced. *Confession. Algonkin. Children. Vengeance.* She wasn't busy enough.

The chandelier was finally rewired, re-hung with crystals, and bolted back onto the ceiling. At six o'clock, with the family and everyone else still working in the house gathered in the entrance hall, it burst into glory. There were cheers and applause.

The phone in the study rang while everyone was still laughing and clapping. Linnet, near the front door, saw Mark, on the far side of the hall, dart into the south corridor. The ringing stopped. A minute later he reappeared, caught her eye, flicked his eyes at the front door, and walked quietly around. They slipped out the door one after the other and eased it shut behind them.

They headed down the road, late afternoon sunlight flaring in their eyes as the trees bent and waved. "That was Mr. Urban. He said Chantal phoned him and asked him to pass on a message, that we should come and get our email. She thinks we'd like to see it right away."

Chapter 31

LINNET'S HEART WAS THUMPING double-quick when they arrived at the *Leader* office, and not just from 20 minutes of race-walking. Mark printed off the covering email and the attachment, a single page each, waved goodbye and thanks to Norris, and they were on the street again. He stopped in the middle of the pavement and ran his eyes over the cover note. Linnet read silently over his arm.

> Hi, Mark and Linnet. So you did it! I wonder how you persuaded Dell. Maybe I'd better not ask. I owe you. This letter fills the gap in the story. Thank you!
>
> Transcribing the letter was not difficult. I've read other documents from the same time period and I'm familiar with the script, and the style of French used then. The translation I've sent you is a first draft, but it's accurate. It seemed to me you should have it as soon as possible.
>
> I had suspected something bad, but even so this broke my heart. Don't let it break yours. Chantal

"Here's the attachment." Mark pulled out the second page.

Linnet turned away. "I don't want to read it." Her stomach hurt.

"I do. I need to know." A cluster of hikers shouldered past, leaning under gigantic packs. Mark folded both pages in four and stuck them in a back pocket of his jeans. "I'll read it somewhere else."

The wind was getting up as they climbed the winding road to Lynx Leap. Dust eddies blew into their faces. The hazy sunlight shuttered off and on as the trees swayed. "Alicia will be on pins and needles." Mark smiled up at the scudding clouds. "If the weather turns really bad, nobody will come to the party."

How could he be so calm with that letter in his pocket? As if everything was normal. *Broke my heart.* A letter like a bomb that could blow up when it was opened and shatter you. She decided when they got there she would go straight into the house and leave him to it, and make him promise not to tell her anything.

Dark thoughts clawed up from deep inside. All the bad things that could happen to children. To girls, thirteen. *I'm thirteen.*

Somebody said: "Here, I think." She looked up and around, startled. Mark put a hand on her arm. "You okay?"

"Oh. Sure." She pushed back the hair that kept blowing into her face. "Where.... Oh, right."

They stood in a cleared spot near the brink of the gorge, downriver from the fury of the Jaws. Trees screened them on the side nearest the road. On the other side, a narrow path ran close to the edge of the cliff. Upriver, a corner of the roof of Lynx Leap poked through the trees.

"I'm stopping here," Mark said. "Any closer, and Fleabites might spot us and come stick his nose in." He watched her with the wary look she'd seen once or twice before. "You staying or going?"

"I don't want...." *But nothing real could possibly be as bad as what I've been imagining. Could it?* "I'm staying. I need to know, too."

"Okay, good. I'll read it out loud. Then you can read it again if you want to." He gave her another wary look, then read:

> My dear son Alain: This is a confession. You have already heard the story of how I led a company to the north, long ago; how when we came into conflict with the Algonkin we defeated them utterly; and

198

how, later, we were ourselves routed by an unseen enemy, and fled to the south.

You do not know the real reason I fled. Today I confessed this thing to my parish priest. He directed me, as partial penance, to make the story known to you; for a large part of my sin, he said, was that I kept it secret, and for so many years.

You know that I am not an evil man, and that I try to deal justly with my fellows. But on that day long ago I did an evil thing. The act arose from fear, which clouded my judgment.

This is what happened. You know that when battle threatened, I sent men to take prisoner any people left in the Algonkin village, to hold them as hostages. They found a group of twelve: two babes in arms, eight children of between perhaps four and ten years, and two girls of perhaps thirteen years. These were led to a place in the river gorge, in the cliff wall across from that out-thrust stone that the Algonkin called sacred, but lower down, where a crevice led to a small cave. The hostages were obliged to enter the cave. The native holy man was put in with them.

You will imagine that, after the enemy was defeated, we would have freed the hostages, for they were no longer of any use to us. And so we would have done, had the battle ended differently. But it seemed to me that our victory had been so complete, ending in the deaths of 43 Algonkin warriors, some only boys, and women also, that reports of the bloodbath, for such it was, would bring allied bands to attack us in revenge. Such reports could be carried by the remaining Algonkins: the hostages.

I contrived, then, that they would carry no tales. I, with my two aides, went secretly at night and sealed the entrance of the cave with large stones. Before the entrance was completely sealed, we heard the holy man chanting. I could not understand his language, but I believe to this day that he was uttering a curse and a promise of vengeance. I believe it because of what followed.

I ordered my two aides to keep this action secret. I did not tell Fr. Laplace, our Jesuit. My aides were among those later killed by the unseen drummer. I was left alone to suffer guilt and bad dreams for the rest of my long life.

At the time of the act I believed I had no choice: it was necessary to ensure the survival of my company. Yet even then I knew it was a black evil: the murder of helpless children. I confess it now, for I will die soon and I do not wish to go to God with that stain on my soul.

My son, I direct you to preserve this account, and your descendants also. I do not know when this sin of mine will ever come to light, and into the common knowledge of men, but I believe that some day it must do so.

My dear son, I trust you will forgive me and remember me with affection, as I do you.

Silence fell. Then Mark cleared his throat. "Well, that's...." His voice faded.

So that's what I've been hearing. The children's voices, the crying. Linnet. Linnet. Calls for help. Me help! What could I do? Push the stones away? Too late.

How did they—those girls, same age as me—how did they comfort the little ones? They sang. Of course, that accounts for it—the singing. They sang to comfort them, to make them not afraid, only it didn't work.

"Linnet!"

She blinked away tears. Mark had his fists around both her wrists. "I should never have got you involved in this. You can't take it."

"And you can?"

"It was awful," he said gently. "But it was a long time ago. It's in the past. We can't do anything about it now." He gave her hands a shake. "But Chantal can: she can make sure the truth comes out. Just like Lot wanted. Doesn't that help?"

"Not a lot." She pulled her hands away. Red drops fell on her sweater.

"What the hell?" He grabbed her right hand. She pulled away again and looked. A bracelet of shining crimson circled her wrist. She sat down on the ground as her legs folded up by themselves. Mark dropped to his knees in front of her. "Linnet!"

"It's okay, it's not as bad as it looks. I just don't like blood much. Makes me sickish."

"It's that scratch from the lamp. You've been rubbing on it."

"I have not!" She turned her wrist over. "That scratch was only on one side. This goes all the way around. It's a message, except I'm not sure what it means."

"I don't get you, not a word." He stood up. "Come on, let's get you in and fixed up."

"Wait." She stayed on the ground. "I don't want people asking questions. Can't face them."

He thought a moment, then nodded. "Okay, back in half a sec. Don't fall over the cliff."

He was back in ten minutes. Long enough for Linnet to slow her breath, calm her stomach, and force her whirling thoughts into some kind of order. They weren't any less horrendous. Her wrist stopped bleeding, but her heart still hurt.

Mark wrapped her wrist in a dozen layers of gauze, then taped the ends. She wobbled to her feet, shook the overlong sleeve of her sweater down over the gauze, and followed him along the narrow path.

The growl of the Jaws grew louder. Mist blew in their faces. They rounded a bend and Lynx Leap rose ahead, springing straight up from the brink like an extension of the cliff. Opposite, the original Lynx Leap jutted out, as if reaching to touch the house.

Linnet shouted over the roar of white water. "Remember what Dumas said in his letter, about the sacred rock? There it is, the Leap." Her eyes scanned the cliff face below the house. It was gouged and cracked and fissured in a dozen places, some of the cracks dribbling small streams. She pointed. "That must be where it happened."

"What? You mean...." Mark stared at the cliff face.

"The hostages. Somewhere down there below the house."

The river snarled and writhed like a dragon. Or a giant lynx. Something alive yet mythical. You could see horns and claws in the jetting froth. No wonder this had been holy ground. Linnet shivered and stepped back from the edge.

"I think I see where this is leading us." Mark pushed through the brush toward the road. "And I think I know what Uncle Lot meant in that note we found in the skunk. He said there was danger. As if we might do something, like light a fuse to set things off again."

"Somebody did light the fuse. Not us, somebody else."

Mark searched her face and tried to grin. "You think you see a pattern."

She nodded. "So do you, only you won't admit it."

"Well, okay, there are some really weird repetitions." He stuck hands in pockets, elaborately at ease. "It seems to have started with that thing in 1670. Shaman gets his hand cut off, the French take those twelve hostages and ... uh."

"Yeah."

"And then twelve French get massacred, hands cut off. Okay, you can see why it happened that time. Somebody took revenge. Obvious." He rocked on his feet, back and forth. "But it happens again later. In 1820 and 1892, same numbers, same modus operandi. Why? Once wasn't enough? That's the big question. Who and why?"

"I think I know who. For sure we know why."

"No, we don't."

"Yes! What started it? Each time, somebody was murdered. Somebody who couldn't fight back. Like those twelve kids."

Mark dug his hands deeper and swung away. Linnet stuck to him. "1820. That mill owner's wife and son. 1892. Violet Tanner. And this year, Lot."

"Whoa!" He spun around, furious, but underneath was fear. "That's crap!"

"And each time, the first murders happened at Lynx Leap, or on the spot it would be. Right above where those children went into the cave."

Mark turned his back and tramped on up the road, shaking his head. She ran after him.

"Don't you see it? That's what lights the fuse!" She stabbed a finger at the house. "When somebody spills innocent blood *right there*!"

Chapter 32

MARK HUNCHED his shoulders. "Okay, okay! There's a pattern. I see it. I can't explain it. I don't know what to think."

Linnet trudged beside him. "Who can we tell?"

"Who would listen? Theo? My dad? I'm not sure I believe it myself."

"It's going to happen, Mark. He's awake."

"He? Who?"

She held up her gauze-wrapped wrist. He laughed, not convincingly. There was nothing more to say.

They slogged on up to the house. The decorator's van and a pickup with ladders on the side were on their way down. They passed with cheerful toots of their horns. Mark waved.

He laughed suddenly. "No, I still can't believe it! All this about a revenge-crazed lynx-ghost-medicine man, if that's what you've got in mind. I just can't swallow it!"

"So it's all in my head?"

"Well, no." He flicked a hand vaguely. "But I'll bet there's a natural explanation, if we only look. There always is, right? And no part of me thinks we're about to see mass murder in Lynx Delving."

Linnet looked at him hopelessly. If Mark wasn't convinced, what chance did she have of making anyone else listen?

Now was the time to leave. Now, before it began. The wish filled her to bursting, but only for a moment. Then: Yeah, and leave Mark alone to face what comes? No, running away wasn't among the choices. Even if she could.

They crossed the clearing, now a gravelled parking lot, and pushed open the front door. Mark took a deep breath. "Wow. I can't believe this is the same place!"

The entrance hall smelled of wax polish and flowers. In one corner stood big pots of wild asters and ferns, backed by tall mirrors. "That's where they're putting the musicians tonight," Mark looked around approvingly. "I can't see any ghoulies lurking here, can you?"

The hall, once so dark, was full of light. The chandelier blazed. Bright rugs stretched across the scoured stone floor. Sofas and chairs stood around invitingly.

"You think a good scrubbing and a coat of paint will scare this thing away?" Linnet thought of the leaking cellar below this floor, and below that the night world of tunnels and cracks and secret cavities. And whatever lay hidden there. "Somehow I don't think it'll be enough."

BY EIGHT O'CLOCK that evening, Lynx Leap was alive with music and colour. Men in light summer suits and women in bright dresses thronged what Alicia had taken to calling the great hall, strolled the corridors and clustered in the gallery (study) and lounge (parlour).

Operation Makeover was a success. Alicia was coolly radiant as she circulated, pointing out the unique beauties of the house. Dell, slender and perfect in long-sleeved black silk, guided reeves, councillors and chamber of commerce members to the buffet in the gallery/study.

Jacob took real estate agents on tours of the main rooms. Linnet thought his cheerful smile looked strained.

She wandered restlessly among the crowd, listening, watching, nibbling and wishing she had some job to do. She had offered, but

Dell had looked her over and asked if she had something to wear that made her look less like a waif from *Les Mis*.

Linnet looked down at herself. "This is the only dress I brought with me." It was a high-waisted denim thing with deep pockets in the full skirt. "What's wrong with it?"

"Not a thing. Just stay out of the way, please."

Wandering into the kitchen, which was quiet because the catering staff were busy elsewhere, she found Mark. He stood at the closed door to the cellar, grumbling as he sorted through a handful of keys. He was irritable because Alicia had insisted that he put on a suit, white shirt and tie. "And the only suit I have is this one I wore to the funeral. I feel like an undertaker's apprentice."

"You look nice. Nicer than me. I look like a waif, whatever that is. What are you doing?"

"Dad wants me to lock this door. We don't want people poking around down there."

"Problem?" Linnet opened the door a crack. Trickling sounds and a strong smell of damp drifted up.

"The usual, only more so. A look at the cellar would spoil the wonderful delusion we're trying to create." He pawed through the clinking handful. "I've got all the keys in the house, including the ones I found, and none of them fit."

"Guess you'll have to sit on guard." She nodded at a chair, only half paying attention. The smell of the cellar made her nervous. So did the rhythm that was juddering, barely audible, under and a beat off from the smooth melodies floating from the five-man jazz combo in the great hall. "Mark? Do you hear anything ... um ... different?"

"No. What should I hear?"

"Oh, nothing." He wouldn't. The mood he was in now, it was a waste of breath to mention her worries. He was all nerves and brittleness.

He dropped down on the chair next to the cellar door. "Do me a favour, will you? Get me some of those goodies? I can put up with boredom but not starvation."

In the crowded study, Linnet found a plate and heaped it with sausage rolls, chicken wings, crackers and cheese. Bullets of conversation hit her from all sides.

"...marvellous how they've brightened up the old ruin."

"...let it go for a quarter million."

"...like a look at the foundations, though."

"...see it as a resort lodge. Hunting, rafting, hiking..."

"...funny smell..."

"...must be the site, right on the river."

"...adore that chandelier!"

After the last comment came a prolonged flickering of lights. The room crawled with shadows, dimming the sparkle of crystal and silver. The buzz of conversation faltered.

Out of the corner of her eye, Linnet saw something rise in a corner and slink under a mahogany sideboard. She froze.

Then the lights steadied and voices rose again. Somebody said, "Generator, yes? Looks like it's not all it should be."

There was nothing under the sideboard when Linnet bent and looked. The flickering lights were playing tricks with her eyes, creating shadows for her imagination to shape. She picked up the loaded plate and carried it carefully out of the study and across the entrance hall, circling around knots of people.

The stones vibrated under her feet. Could be the river. But it was too regular. It pulsed against her soles like the beat of a buried heart. So it must be the musicians, then. The drummer.

But that wasn't their beat.

She stopped in the middle of the hall. On the other side, near the mouth of the north corridor, a tattered figure stood staring at her. Torn T-shirt and tangled hair hanging over his eyes: he was blatantly out of place in this dressy mob. People near him glanced uneasily, pretended they hadn't, and stepped away.

Boyd slipped out of sight. Linnet pushed through the crowd after him, not worrying now about her loaded plate. When she reached the corridor, he was gone. He wasn't in the kitchen, either. Neither was Mark. She dumped Mark's dinner onto the table and snatched up the newly installed phone extension. Theo's number, where... She ran a finger down a printed list taped to the wall.

She was halfway through dialing when she realized there was no dial tone. The phone was dead.

"Well, after all, what could Theo do?" All the same, the breakdown frightened her. So did the flickering of the lights, and the cellar smell of wet earth and mildewed stone that was getting stronger minute by minute.

Lynx Leap was ready to come apart. And Boyd being there was part of it.

Wondering where Mark was, Linnet walked back to the hall, where the crowd grew thicker and noisier as more people arrived. Now you could hardly hear the musicians, though the pulsing offbeat came through clearer than ever.

She pushed through to the staircase and climbed to the third step to look out over the crowd. No sign of Mark. Alicia was at the door, welcoming another cluster of guests. Rain and wind blew in with them, plucking at skirts and snatching at hair.

Looking out over the sea of heads, it hit her. What a chance for revenge! Was this what he'd been waiting for? A gathering of warm bodies in Lynx Leap? If so, his moment had come.

208

The scene below was like a nightmare. Nothing was normal. Not the light, dulling to bronze as the chandelier flickered and dimmed. Not the clashing voices, harsh as crows now and torn by shrill laughter.

The sound and smell of the river seeped back in, overpowering the odours of food and fresh paint and new curtains. Another smell came with it. Musky, wild: an animal smell.

It was beginning.

Chapter 33

LINNET SPOTTED JACOB in the crowd below. As she started down the stairs toward him, it seemed to her that every shadow in the hall held a denser shadow. And all the shadows were moving.

"Mr. Tanner!"

He looked around sharply. The creases between his eyebrows smoothed out when he saw who it was. "Not too bored, I hope, Linnet?"

"Mr. Tanner, you...." What could she say that would convince him? *If you don't call off the party, twelve people will die horribly. Maybe you among them.*

"Linnet? What's wrong?"

"The ... the cellar. It's bad, isn't it?"

"Well, it's not good." He lowered his voice as people nearby turned their heads to listen. "But why should that bother you?"

"Don't you think you should get everybody to leave?" She tried to sound reasonable, but her voice quavered. "I mean, it—it could be dangerous. Suppose there's a cave-in!"

He laughed. "If the house was about to pitch into the gorge, do you think I'd be standing here waiting for it to happen?"

People chuckled. Jacob smiled tightly, gripped Linnet by the shoulder and steered her back toward the stairs.

"No more about the cellar, please!" he whispered. "Unless you want to ruin our show!"

"It's not really about the cellar." She gazed up desperately into his face, so kind and sensible and so much like Mark's. Mark didn't believe either, not even after all they'd learned, not even after what he'd seen with his own eyes.

"Linnet, what's your trouble?" Jacob asked gently.

"I'm afraid."

"Afraid! Of what?"

"Can't you feel it? Don't you hear it?"

"Linnet, I'm sorry. I don't know what you mean."

"The drums! They've been beating since Lot was killed. It means more people are going to die."

When he just shook his head at her, she grabbed his hand and placed it on the banister. The wood thrummed like a cello.

He smiled. "That's just the river."

"No, listen! Even your sister can hear it now. Look, she thinks the band's doing it."

Alicia was speaking to the band leader. From across the room they could see her curt gestures. The man threw his hands in the air. The others put down their instruments. But the off-beat throbbed on. Now it was a soft boom you could hear over the babble of the crowd.

"Where's Mark?" Jacob asked suddenly.

"I don't know." Linnet looked around anxiously.

"I sent him for his camera ten minutes ago. I asked him to take pictures of the party."

"It shouldn't take him ten minutes to get his camera."

"Try to find him, will you?" He smiled at her crookedly. "I don't think for a moment there's anything wrong. But I'll just go and check the cellar again."

Linnet watched him edge politely through the crowd towards the corridor leading to the kitchen. So she'd told Jacob. What else could she do? Climb on a chair and scream warnings? They'd think she'd gone bonkers!

211

Mark. Where was he? Not knowing where he'd gone worried her, for no reason she could name, almost as much as knowing Boyd was lurking around the house.

At that moment she felt someone standing behind her. Before she could turn, a hand touched her shoulder and sharp nails dug in.

No, not nails. Claws, curved and razor-sharp.

With a choked cry she whirled around and fell back. Then caught her balance and stood trembling. Felix whooped. "Wow! You jumped a mile! Ever think of trying out for the Olympics, Linnet?"

"You creep! You've been messing in my room!" She snatched at the mummified hand.

He hid it behind his back. "This thing would make a great Halloween prop. What's it from, a cougar?"

"Gimme that!" She darted around him, but he backed away and moved the paw to his other hand. Some of the guests looked at them and laughed.

"You think we're playing games," she whispered fiercely. "But you're wrong. There's just one game going on here tonight. And none of us is playing."

He narrowed his eyes at her. "You all right? You sound funny."

"I'm just fine, thank you." She flashed him a bright smile. "Considering some of us are about to die."

"What're you babbling about?" For a moment he forgot what he was holding. Linnet lunged, grabbed it, and sprang up the stairs. He leaped after her, giggling. She whirled on the fourth step and held the hand poised, claws reaching for his face.

Felix held her eyes; his own eyes widened. He opened and closed his mouth, and stepped back. He backed down the stairs, holding the banister, eyes on her face, as if scared she might come after him. At the bottom he whirled and darted away.

Linnet ran up the stairs and collapsed on the landing, out of sight of the people in the hall. She dropped the paw on the floor as if it was burning her.

What had Felix seen in her face, that moment she'd turned on him? Something that scared the nonsense clean out of him.

It was the first time she had ever touched the mummified paw with her bare hand. At that moment, something like an electric shock had blazed through her. Only it wasn't electricity. It was more like recognition. Like the jolt of memory that comes with a whiff of long-forgotten odour, dragging with it a mob of emotions.

Fury, grief, horror. They'd sent her flying up the stairs with a need to burn off that blistering energy, or burst. She crouched a moment on the first step above the landing, listening to the drumbeat from below, feeling it in the step under her, and looking at the mummified paw, which seemed to crawl on the wood of the landing. The last thing she wanted to do was touch it again.

But she had to. Had to know what it could tell. Its emotions burst from inside her, but they weren't hers. She breathed evenly a minute or two, long enough to calm her heartbeat. Then reached down and picked it up.

Not an electric jolt this time, now that she had some inkling of how it would be. More like a hurricane. Rage that could break stone. Grief that could tear the sky. *The children.* Hatred, the need to repay, an acid burning through her brain, changing her. *Monster.* And beneath all, an ocean of weariness and despair.

Linnet opened her eyes and dropped the clawed hand into one of the deep pockets of her denim dress. She clasped her trembling hands on her knees until she judged she might be able to stand up without falling down again.

A flicker of movement at the top of the stairs caught her eye. She

213

looked up, but nothing was there. "Mark?" No answer. She stood and climbed on up.

The second-floor corridor was deserted, but not quiet. The beat that was growing audible downstairs was a deep, hollow drumming up here. Linnet hesitated, then walked towards the north end of the corridor. Mark's room was the last.

Maybe he was having trouble with his camera. Or maybe he'd forgotten where he put it. Maybe it was as simple as that.

But the lights were blinking and cracks were zigzagging down the freshly painted walls. A picture, newly hung, slid down and crashed, peppering her with bits of glass. This was not a time when Mark would be sitting on his bed playing with the controls on his camera.

The door to his room stood partly open. It was dark in there. She reached in to flip the light switch. A hand gripped her wrist. She gasped and pulled back but couldn't wrench free.

"Never mind the light," Boyd whispered. His voice had always sounded as if it didn't get enough use, but now it was the rustle of a dry leaf.

"Let go of me!" She yanked with all her strength, but Boyd's one remaining hand might have been made of iron.

"I won't hurt you. It's Mark."

"What've you done to him?"

"Not me. Come on." Boyd pushed out of the room and dragged her towards the door to the stairwell that led to the third floor.

Linnet dug in her heels. "Let me go right now or I'll scream my head off!"

In the flickering light, he looked ghastly. He had lost weight, his torn shirt hanging on him in dirty folds. His eyes stared from hollow sockets. He looked like what Theo believed him to be: a borderline nutcase with shady connections. Yet Linnet had never feared him. She didn't fear him now. All she felt for him was pity.

"Let me go," she said more gently, "and I'll listen."

His grip loosened. "You got to stop what's happening."

"Me? Stop it? How?"

"You got to! That's why we were chosen, you and me. Marked." He held up his bandaged stump. "But not killed. Because we can hear the drums and he thinks we can do something. He wants it to end."

"I know. But how can I end it if you couldn't?"

He sagged against the wall. "Then we're dead."

"Look, tell me something I can do. Where's Mark?"

The lights dimmed nearly to nothing. Boyd flinched. "Up there." He pointed at the ceiling with his stump.

Plaster popped and a crack ran down the wall. "If he's up there, we've got to get him down! The house isn't safe any more."

"It never was safe," Boyd whispered.

This time it was Linnet who hurried ahead, with Boyd scuffing at her heels, up the narrow stairs. Halfway up, he caught her arm. "Sh!"

"What?" she whispered.

He licked his lips, pale and frightened. Or was it fright? Maybe it was anticipation. *Maybe I'm being a very big fool. Maybe I'd better get out of here just as fast as I can.*

A moment later the light that radiated up the stairs from the second floor went out, and Linnet's moment of choice was gone.

Chapter 34

"BETTER HURRY," came Boyd's dry-leaf voice from the darkness.

Linnet looked upward. A dull yellow glow outlined the door at the top. That meant Mark, or someone, was up there with a flashlight.

It took Linnet only seconds to figure out that whoever was up there, she stood a better chance of escaping from the attic, if she had to, than of fighting off Boyd in this stairwell.

Careful not to make a sound, she climbed to the top and eased the door open.

The thunder of the gorge burst out at them. The pounding beat was overwhelming here, shaking the silhouettes of deer antlers against the flashlight glow. The sound battered Linnet's chest. She was suffocating. She forced herself to breathe.

At least there was no need to worry about making a noise. She could stomp like a bison and nobody would hear.

The light seemed to be fixed near the centre of the room. Linnet worked her way slowly towards it, all the while aware of large pieces of furniture looming and shaking above her. As she edged around a dresser piled high with cardboard cartons, she felt the massive thing creak and shift. The topmost carton slid from the pile and crashed to the floor, scattering books. Someone called out sharply. Linnet crouched down in the shadow of the dresser, tucking her robe in around her feet. Boyd settled behind her: she couldn't hear him but she could smell him.

A metre away, almost close enough to touch, Mark stood squinting against a bright light. She saw his face in profile. He was standing stiffly, his back braced against one of the posts that held up the roof beams. What was he doing? Why was his face fixed in that strange, tight mask?

She opened her mouth to call out to him, but Boyd gripped her elbow and hissed "Wait!"

"How many times do I have to say it?" Mark shouted over the pounding beat. "There's nothing here!"

So he wasn't alone. The light swayed, then steadied, as if someone had set it down. A second figure stepped in front of it. The silhouette was slender. The edges of the hair caught the light and made a golden halo around the black shape of the head. Felix?

Mark strained forward, and then Linnet saw that he wasn't leaning against the post. He was tied to it. His arms were pulled behind him and what looked like an old clothesline was cinched tight around his waist and legs.

Keeping an eye on the golden-haired silhouette, she slipped around the corner of the dresser and crouched down in the shadow of the stuffed black bear. The move brought her close enough to reach out and touch the post.

It also brought her to a position where, if she eased her head around the bear's shaggy flank, she could see the anonymous figure's face. Linnet stared in shock.

It was Dell.

Her body, sheathed in black, was invisible. Her pale head and hands seemed to float in the dark. She wore her usual look of cool calm. "Stop thrashing about. I'm out of patience. I want answers and I want them now."

One hand held something that reflected the light in a long leaf shape. It was a knife: the obsidian knife from Lot's study.

"I've been all over this house, top to bottom." Dell's clear voice

217

cut through the boom of the river. "I've looked in every single book in the library. I've searched the archives. I've scoured Lot's computer. I even opened those disgusting dead things in the study. So it has to be here."

"Go ahead. Waste your time."

"No, there's too much up here for me to go through it all. Besides, why should I? You're going to tell me. Where did he hide that money?"

Linnet suppressed a gasp. So that's what she'd been doing. Not just taking inventory. Dell the beautiful, the perfect. Dell the efficient, who worked so hard and always did the right thing. Dell, with her steel-trap mind, focused on the bottom line.

The bottom line. Guess that should've clued us in.

"For the last time—"

"Don't give me that again! Of course you know where it is. Lot told you. You were always his favourite, God knows why. He hid a message for you, somewhere here, and you found it."

"You saw what we found. You read it."

"That was a red herring. Or a code. He got a message to you somehow. And now you're going to tell me what it said."

She moved closer and placed the point of the knife under his chin. He pulled back against the post. The corners of her mouth lifted to show beautifully whitened teeth. It was the first real smile Linnet had seen on Dell's face. She didn't like it.

"Feel that, Mark? I'll use it if I have to. I'm not sentimental."

"What ... what happened to Lot?" Mark sounded short of breath. "Did he ... get in your way?"

"He caught me taking some of the silverware," she said casually. "I needed the money, and of course he'd never miss the things. But he threatened to have me arrested. Can you believe it? Me, his own

218

flesh and blood! Arrested!"

Mark's hands clenched against the clothesline that bound them. "So you killed him."

"I just gave him a push. He fell down the cellar stairs. I had no other choice. Couldn't let him turn me in, could I?"

Linnet had never liked Dell but she'd envied Dell's style. Always polished, perfect, in command. Linnet had wished she could be so poised. Had wanted to be like her, in that way.

And Dell had murdered an old man for his money. Nausea pushed up in her throat and she swallowed it down.

Mark's hands clenched again. He was trying to work the knots loose, and not having much effect. *Suppose I just reach out and....*

No. Dell was too close, and facing this way. She might see. And she could use that knife on Mark before Linnet could free him.

Go for help? That would take too long.

I'll have to tackle her. But with what? What would serve as a shield against that knife? She looked around but saw nothing useful except a book, lying on the floor behind her.

She picked it up, looked at it and bit back a slightly hysterical laugh. Gold letters winked from the dusty cover. *Treasure Island.*

"Where is it, Mark? Don't make me work at this!"

"Dell, you're crazy. There is no money!"

"You're lying."

The knife turned, its edges winking. Mark's breath hissed in. At the same moment the beat of the gorge swelled to a thundering roar.

Now! Linnet's fingers tightened around the book. Before she could move, floorboards creaked behind her and a hand shoved her face against the bear. Dell snapped out a word.

When Linnet pulled herself upright, two figures were tussling on the floor. She lunged at the post where Mark was tied and tore at the knots. They were hard and the rope was stiff. She yanked desperately.

The struggling figures went still. The drumbeat stopped. Silence fell so suddenly and so totally that Linnet thought she had gone deaf. Her fingers froze on the knots.

Boyd's bulk moved. Linnet let out her breath. "It's over, thank God! Now we can get out of here."

But Boyd didn't get up. Dell pushed him aside and rose gracefully, the knife still in her hand. Boyd's body lay at her feet like a blood sacrifice before a goddess.

Chapter 35

DELL BRUSHED DUST from her dress before glancing at Mark and Linnet. "So now there's two of you. What a bore." She didn't look at Boyd.

"Linnet, run!" Mark muttered.

"She knows better than that. Don't you, Linnet? Long before you could convince anybody to come up here, Mark would be dead. I'd be oh, so upset, his taking his own life like that. And who would take your word against mine?" Dell smiled sweetly.

Linnet could only give a fraction of her attention to what Dell was saying. While her fingers still tugged at the ropes holding Mark, three-quarters of her mind was on edge for what was happening all around.

Something was taking shape in the darkness of the attic. Something monstrous. She could hear it, smell it, almost see it.

Lot's murder had wakened it from sleep. It had been prowling for days, tasting blood, building its strength. And the moment Dell killed Boyd, it had broken free.

The rank, wild smell of fur filled Linnet's senses. The attic was full of pattering and rustling. Something moved at the edge of the light: a tail flicked, an eye tooth gleamed.

She made one last grasp at rationality. The vibrations were doing it. The floor was shaking, making the stuffed menagerie shift around.

"All right, let's have it." Dell stepped forward briskly. "I'm tired of this. You, girl—"

She didn't finish. She looked over Linnet's shoulder and her eyes widened, the green irises vanishing to black. Her lips moved. *No.*

The pattering and rustling swelled to a storm. Dell backed, turned and took one step.

The floor tilted under Linnet's feet. She threw her arms around the post, and around Mark's waist. A wardrobe fell over with a thunderous crash. Glass tinkled.

Dell sprawled. The obsidian knife jolted from her hand and skidded across the floorboards to Linnet's feet. She scooped it up and started sawing at the rope.

A cold snout prodded her leg. It was the black bear. It slid past her, its clawed feet scraping. Then the gutted deer went by, still trailing cotton.

"We're slanting!" Mark yelled. "The floor's collapsing! Linnet, get out!"

Still hugging the post with one arm, she went on doggedly sawing.

The flashlight fell from where Dell had propped it and rolled to and fro across the floor. The stuffed animals jumped and jolted past through the crazed light.

It was the light, Linnet told herself. It had to be the light that made them look alive.

A coyote's grey back arched as it sprang. A moose curveted grotesquely, its antlers scything the air. A wolverine's black lips wrinkled back from yellow fangs. The cougar flowed by, head low, tail lashing.

Body after body hurtled past. Showers of birds. Bats like scraps of midnight. Somewhere in the storm of hoofs and claws and teeth, Dell screamed.

The floor tilted again. And then, with a sound like a mountain collapsing into a valley, everything slid. Chairs and tables sailed by, broken legs spearing the air. A massive walnut dresser spun past slowly on its ceramic knobs, just missing Mark's knees.

The first of the cords parted. Linnet yanked at the others. Just as Mark pulled free, the flashlight went flying again and then went out.

The uproar grumbled into not-quite-silence. From all around came the groan of timber. The river soughed like wind, no longer booming.

Linnet couldn't make herself let go of the post, the only firm anchor in this chaos. "What happened?"

Mark was wrapped around it too. "The house. It's coming away from the cliff."

"We've got to get out!"

"Yeah."

"What about Dell?"

"I've got a feeling...."

"Me too."

Mark filled his lungs and yelled Dell's name, but there was no answer. He reached around and unwrapped Linnet's hands from the post. "Get going!"

She started scrambling up the sloping floor. Mark was not right behind her. She stopped, looked. The darkness was almost total. "Mark!"

"I have to get Dell!" he called from the darkness.

The floor jolted, sank, and stopped again. "There's no time!"

"Go!"

"Not without you!"

He yelled again. "Dell!"

Down slope, the darkness tore with a crash. Rain blew in. "The outer wall's gone!" Mark shouted.

Then he was at her side, a hand on her shoulder, pushing her forward. It was like scaling an unstable hillside in an earthquake. Toppled furniture and heaps of boxes, black on black, tumbled across their way. Books slithered underfoot like loose stones.

Once, breathless, Linnet stopped and held Mark back. "What's that sound?"

A footstep. Then, after a long pause, another. Glass crunched.

"Dell?" Mark called.

"Too heavy." Linnet tugged at his arm. They scrambled on. Mark found the end wall by ramming his hand into it. They felt along the wall to the door, which was off its hinges, and started down the stairs, awkward and crabwise on the skewed steps.

Something grabbed Linnet's skirt and she sat down with a thump. The cloth tore when she pulled at it. She touched a jagged piece of railing that had just missed impaling her thigh.

Mark thumped down beside her. "I should've stayed."

"And get yourself killed?"

"I should've risked it."

"No. Come on."

The stairs wound down forever in the dark. They reached the doorway to the second floor and paused for breath. Cracking noises came from the walls.

"We'll be buried alive. Or dead." Linnet didn't know she'd said it aloud until Mark spoke.

"We've made it this far. We'll make it all the way."

He started down again, kicking debris aside. Linnet paused to look back and up. Something was watching her from higher up. In the blackness it was only eyes. Wide-set, narrow, pale golden eyes. Cat's eyes. Then they blinked out.

Whenever it wants me, it's got me.

Cold and trembling, she slithered downward. They reached the doorway to the kitchen. It was closed, and stuck when they pushed at it.

Linnet's heart plunged. "Somebody locked it!"

"It's only blocked." Mark shoved with his shoulder. "Come on, heave!"

They strained against it. A dead weight on the other side gave way grudgingly. Mark forced the opening wider and they climbed through over what felt like the new refrigerator lying on its back, open. Things squished and crunched underfoot. The aroma of bacon-wrapped scallops rose.

Linnet skidded on something slimy and saved herself by grabbing Mark's arm. "I think that was your dinner."

They reached the corridor. Mark laughed aloud. "Home stretch!"

Behind them, in the kitchen, wood shrieked. It sounded as if giant hands were tearing the door from its hinges.

They grabbed hands and ran, stumbling and kicking debris at every stride. A few metres ahead, the archway to the entrance hall shaped a tall grey oval. Mortar showered from the arch. A stone fell.

Soft and heavy came the steps behind. Nearer now. What had she told Felix? A game. They were part of a game it was playing. Cat and mice.

The floor jolted again. Mark yelled and sprawled. Linnet stumbled over the six-inch crack that had just opened in the floor. She yanked at his arm. He lurched up and they clung together, burst out of the corridor into the hall.

The front door stood open. White light streamed through from outside, lighting up a swath of crushed flowers and broken glass.

Linnet glanced back. The mouth of the corridor behind them filled with a shadowy shape. "It's right behind!"

"I know!" Mark yanked at her arm. Their run became a mad

dash: skidding on the smeared floor, tripping where the stones jutted up askew, dodging and leaping over overturned sofas and chairs.

The doorway was only a few strides ahead. They saw now that the white light was a row of car headlights aimed at the house. Against the glare figures were waving and shouting.

"Almost there!" Mark laughed jubilantly. A pace behind, Linnet put on a burst of speed. A jutting flagstone caught her toe and sent her flying. She lay stunned.

The mummified hand, which could have bounced from her pocket at any time during their wild race through the house, now slid out and lay on the floor beside her, claws curled upward as if beckoning.

Mark knelt at her side. "Get up! Hurry!" She struggled to her feet. Then his fingers bit into her arm. "Don't look back."

She didn't have to look. She knew. But since it was too late to run, she turned and looked.

Leaping up the slope towards them was a giant shadow. It grew as it came. And moment by moment, it changed. The snarling mask of the lynx vanished into a silhouette of absolute darkness. Out of the silhouette formed a human face, the eyes black and haggard.

Next moment the human eyes grew narrow and golden, the teeth grew long, the cat swallowed the man. A scream burst from the cat's throat. All within two beats of a labouring heart.

Linnet picked up the clawed hand. It was the only thing she had. She wasn't even sure it was a weapon.

Memories shocked through her. She fought them aside. *Not mine!* But they kept coming, like lightning pouring through her.

Sunlight on river spray. Smoke of cooking fires. Hair flying, eyes bright, children laughing.

The bearded faces. The cave. The light dying, stone by stone.

226

Screaming. Weeping. Singing. The small bodies, tiny hands.
The last counted breaths.
Death. Death. Death.

"Not mine!" Linnet screamed, and hurled the hand into the cat's face.

Chapter 36

MARK WAS YANKING at her arm, urging her towards the open door. Linnet moved. It seemed to her she had been away. Time had passed. How much? An hour, a day. A few centuries.

They sprinted hand in hand to the doorway. Linnet would have rushed straight out, but at the last moment she grabbed the doorframe and teetered there. A metre of blackness gaped between the threshold and the pavement outside.

The house was peeling from the cliff. And taking them with it.

The gap widened. "Jump!" someone screamed.

They leaped. Mark made it with an inch to spare. Linnet's toe gouged the crumbling edge. Hands grabbed her as she slid.

Then she found herself crushed inside the crook of Jacob's left arm. He had Mark tight in the other.

"We thought everyone was out!" His voice was shaking. "Another minute, and...." His grip tightened. Mark coughed. The air was thick with dust. "Everybody back!" Jacob yelled.

They retreated to the far side of the parking lot. Lynx Leap tilted backward, splitting into sections. It fell like a mountain blasted by dynamite, with a theatrical slowness. The earth thundered. Linnet covered her ears.

Clouds of spray spouted from the gorge. The headlights shaped cones of swirling white.

MARK STAYED WITH his father overnight in the Leaping Lynx Motel. Linnet stayed with Theo. She didn't sleep much. Next morning Boyd's body was found in the river, washed up on the rocks downstream. By the time Mark and Linnet walked up from the village, near noon, Dell had still not turned up.

"Alicia keeps saying she just went away." Mark sounded exasperated. "She says Dell has been wanting her own space. How blind can you be?"

"It's what she wants to believe."

"I wish I could believe it."

"Mark." She stopped him and made him look at her. "He wouldn't have let her live. Don't you get that? And if you'd stayed, I'd have stayed too, and he'd have taken us and there'd be three, no, four of us dead."

"I know that. But I'll never feel right about it." They walked on.

They hadn't told anyone what Dell had said and done in the attic. Already Boyd's death was being treated as suicide. As far as most people knew, he was the only casualty.

Jacob, alarmed by what he saw in the cellar that evening, had cleared all the guests from the house before it began seriously breaking up. He gave full credit for that to Linnet.

"So it's all wrapped up," Mark said, still grim. "All over."

She nudged his arm with her shoulder. "Is it? After 300 years, you think all the answers are in?"

"Well, maybe not all."

They came in sight of the place where Lynx Leap used to stand. Across from the now empty space the Leap still jutted out over the Jaws, exactly as it had done when Fr. Laplace saw fit to hold a ceremony of exorcism there.

If only he hadn't done that. And if only Dumas hadn't been so pig-headed. And so scared. And if only....

"So that's where you first saw him? The Leap?"

229

"Yeah." Linnet burrowed her hands under her sweatshirt. Even on a sunny day like this, that memory still iced her all over.

"How come you and Boyd were the only ones who could hear and see him, at least at first? Why not me?" Mark sounded offended.

"Boyd said it: we were chosen." She breathed a laugh. "Don't be jealous. You wouldn't like it."

"But chosen for what?"

"I think ... it sounds crazy, but ... to stop him."

"What makes you think he wanted to be stopped? Endless revenge, wasn't that what he wanted?"

"At first, maybe, yes. But later, I don't think so."

Mark made a noncommittal sound. "Well, here we are."

Theo and Kevin had been up earlier. Until the county officials could come to inspect the collapse, and decide what to do about what it had uncovered, it was closed off with stakes, orange mesh fencing and yellow police tape. Large signs were nailed to trees: DANGER. NO TRESPASS.

Mark climbed over the mesh and held it down for Linnet. "Don't get too close to the edge," she warned. "Theo says more of it could cave in any time." He had brought his camera, with its zoom attachment, but she didn't trust him to keep a safe distance.

He flicked his eyebrows. "Didn't I say right from the start this could happen? And did anybody listen to me?"

"And I bet you won't ever let them forget it."

Nothing was left of Lynx Leap but chunks of masonry strewn in the gorge, not much different from the other grey stones down there. The torrent had scattered everything else. Glass and silver glittered in the deep pools. Downriver, the rocks were clogged with drifts of books, splintered furniture, stuffed animals, and anything else that would float. Jacob was organizing a salvage operation.

At the base of the cliff a hollow gaped roofless and frontless. The fall of the house, and the cliff it stood on, had laid bare the cave and what had been hidden there. It had let the sunlight in, and the river. Water eddied through the bones. Some were still joined up into the scaffolds of human shapes, small ones, clinging together. Others were scattered.

By itself next to the back wall of the cave, as if purposely set apart, lay a larger skeleton. Rags of leather robes still clung to the bones. Linnet stared, then squinted. "Mark, let me have your camera."

He passed it over. "Careful, don't drop it in the gorge." She looped the strap over her head.

The zoom lens brought the scene startlingly close. She found the one set apart and moved down the arm bones to the hand. Studied it. Then moved to the other arm.

She passed the camera back. "Look at the one by itself, at the back. Notice the hands." She stepped away from the edge, feeling lightheaded.

"Well," Mark said after a moment. "I guess it's him. Just got the one hand."

"Look at it closer."

He adjusted the focus, muttered, fiddled with the buttons some more. Then he held very still.

"I ... see." He lowered the camera and looked at her, face pale, eyes dark. "Now you can say you told me so."

"Oh, I'll go easy."

"Funny how it all didn't seem really real, before. But wait till they get that skeleton out! That hand will take some explaining, eh?"

"Better get a photo. We've got to tell Chantal about this."

"Good idea." He raised the camera, focused, clicked. "Now a

231

couple more."

Then they both threw themselves back as the cliff edge crumbled beneath their feet. When the clouds of spray had settled they inched forward cautiously and craned their necks.

"I think you're right," Linnet said. "It's finally over."

The cave was buried, the bones scattered and swallowed by the foaming river.

About the author

PATRICIA BOW lives in Kitchener, Ontario. She has written several other books for young people. To find out more about Patricia and her work, visit www.execulink.com/~thebows/patricia.htm.